INTRIGUE IN SIBERIA

Alexi, his sister Tanya, and their entire family were exiles, sent from Leningrad to Siberia because of their faith; forced to accept second-class citizenship in a country that tolerated no god but the state. But not even that frozen wasteland could crush the spirit of the brave, hardy Christian community whose courage and persistence were an inspiration even to their oppressors. And now Alexi had the greatest opportunity of all: a chance to become a true Christian soldier on a mission too dangerous for an adult to dare!

It was Alexi's chance to serve Christ in the most dangerous mission imaginable: delivering forbidden Bibles to Russian Christians whose precious books had been taken by the authorities.

ALEXI'S
Secret ★ Mission

Anita Deyneka

**Illustrated by
Seymour Fleishman**

David C. Cook Publishing Co.
ELGIN, ILLINOIS—WESTON, ONTARIO

David C. Cook Publishing Co., Elgin, IL 60120
Printed in the United States of America
Library of Congress Catalog Number: 74-29466
ISBN: 0-912692-58-8

Contents

Foreword

Many parents in America would rather have their 13-year-old sons grow beanstalks and climb them than be entrusted with missions as serious and far-reaching as that given to Alexi Makarovitch.

Has Anita Deyneka merely imagined such a stalwart Christian boy in the Soviet Union? No, indeed, for she has been to Russia twice, speaks enough of the language to converse, and has based her fascinating story on true events.

Mrs. Deyneka, who began her career as a schoolteacher of secondary grades, has majored in a study both of Russian history and of modern society in the Soviet Union.

Next to their faith, Russian Christian parents treasure their children more than anything on earth. For them it is vital to bequeath an army of well-trained soldiers of the Cross to an atheistic society where Christianity is relegated to the same status as pornography and where the suppression of the Word of God has official sanction.

In such a culture, children of the U.S.S.R. mature more quickly than their counterparts in North America. Some youngsters see their parents taken to jail—hear the dreaded knock on the door by the secret police inspector—feel the sting of peer rebuke when they attend school without the red kerchief of the Young Communist Pioneer Club.

Tests of faith are a daily ordeal. A believer's quest for a Bible is a never-ending struggle.

Read Alexi's story to your children. My wife and I held our children's keen interest as we read Mrs. Deyneka's first book in the series, *Tanya and the Border Guard,* at our dinner table.

And as *you* read, pray for these fellow believers half a world away. To print Bibles they risk going to jail. For their faith they are willing to suffer persecution.

Can we say the same?

La Canada, Cal.

NORMAN B. ROHRER
EXECUTIVE SECRETARY
EVANGELICAL PRESS ASSOCIATION

EDITOR'S NOTE:

As this book went to press, news reached the West that 200 Soviet secret police and militia raided a hidden Bible printing shop in Latvia. Seven Russian Christians were arrested; 15,000 New Testaments and 19 tons of paper and a printing machine were confiscated.

According to news sources, the secret police had posted a large reward for information leading to the location of the hidden Bible printing shop.

1.

Visitors in the Night

Alexi jumped when he heard the sharp knock on the apartment door. His sister Tanya, hunched over the table studying her science lesson, pushed her thick book aside with an anxious frown.

"Poppa," Alexi glanced tensely at the watch his parents had given him for this thirteenth birthday, "who—who would be coming to visit us this late at night?"

"Perhaps it is just one of the neighbors—maybe old Mrs. Gornuk down the hall wants to borrow some beets to put in her borscht soup," Mr. Makarovitch said, trying to calm his family's fears.

His wife stared at the snow piled high outside on the apartment windowsill. "It is a cold, black night for guests to be calling," Mrs. Makarovitch said, pulling her gray shawl close around her shoulders.

The person at the door pounded again. "That

doesn't sound like Mrs. Gornuk." Poppa rose resolutely from his chair. "But of course we must open the door to our visitor."

Tanya hung back in the corner of the little living room beside the green *feekoos* plant that was almost as tall as a small tree, but Alexi stood by the door. Somehow he felt safer by his father. Hesitantly, Poppa unlatched the apartment door.

Two men whom Alexi had never seen before pushed their way into the apartment. "Comrade Makarovitch?" questioned the first visitor, a heavy man who wore a small, black brimmed hat. The other visitor, a short, shy man in a long coat that reached below his knees, stood silently behind the first man, who thrust the identification card of a KGB secret police officer toward Alexi's father.

"We have come to ask some questions—and to make some suggestions, Comrade Makarovitch." The KGB officer with the black hat spoke confidently, as if what he planned to suggest was so sensible he was sure no one would disagree.

Momma slumped into a chair in the corner of the small room. "Oh, Ivan," she murmured weakly to her husband.

Poppa calmly motioned the men to the couch which was also Alexi's bed. "Please sit down, comrades," he offered politely. "You will excuse the blankets. You see, my son was preparing to go to bed soon."

The short man stayed as if on guard by the door, but the big police officer lowered himself onto Alexi's bed. "Yes," he said, turning to Mr. Makarovitch, "I must have a little chat with you—and your family.

"Comrade Ivan," the police officer said, leaning

forward and addressing Mr. Makarovitch in a friendly voice, "I know that you served in the Red Army. You were stationed near Smolensk, weren't you?"

Mr. Makarovitch nodded.

"The army records at Smolensk indicate that you were a good soldier—a sensible man." The KGB officer spoke approvingly to Alexi's father.

Mr. Makarovitch sat silent, waiting for the officer to continue.

"But when you went to the university, you suddenly changed, comrade." The officer's voice sharpened. "We tried to warn you while you were still a student at the university. Later we tried again to turn you back onto the right path." The officer seemed ready to say more, but he glanced at the children and paused.

"You have not changed, Comrade Makarovitch," he continued. "Now your children are following in your footsteps," the officer said, staring at Alexi. "You and your family are *all* caught in the same foolish fanaticism!"

"You mean because we are Christians?" Poppa asked bluntly.

"Yes, because you are *verruyuschiye*—believers." The KGB officer's smile faded as he turned reproachfully to Mr. Makarovitch. "For ten years the supervisor at the factory has been trying to reform you—you an educated man, an engineer," he chided.

"The supervisor assures me that he has made every effort to help you renounce this unscientific foolishness—this so-called faith in God. But instead of cooperating, you insist on infecting others at the factory with your religion. We cannot understand you. The police officer seemed sincerely perplexed.

The apartment was silent. Alexi prayed silently, "Please, God, help Poppa."

"It is true, comrades," Poppa said. His merry black eyes turned sober. "I do not deny my Creator. I believe in Jesus Christ and I will continue to share my great happiness with others. Let me tell you about Jesus . . ."

But the police officer stood so suddenly, his hat almost fell off. He fixed it firmly on his head. "If that is your decision, Comrade Makarovitch," he said, appearing shaken that Poppa was not persuaded, "the authorities also have come to a decision. There is no more room in Leningrad for your family—a *verruyuschiy* engineer who won't keep quiet!"

Alexi gasped, too terrified to speak—too frightened to imagine what the secret police officer's threatening words might mean. Were they going to take his father away? But the officer said "your family." Would he punish all of them—maybe even put them in prison—just because they were Christians?

"In two days," the officer frowned, "you—all of you—will leave Leningrad forever."

"Thank God we go together," Momma murmured.

Alexi stared past the officer out the frosty window toward Leningrad lying in the darkness below. He thought of the canals that laced the city, the Peter and Paul Fortress Island, the long nights of summer when the sun smiled almost 24 hours in the sky, the icy days of winter when Leningrad looked like a fairyland and the hockey rink filled with skaters, the bright days of spring when believers met in the forest.

"But we can't leave Leningrad!" Alexi exclaimed. "We've always lived here!" Desperately he tried to make the KGB officer understand.

"When you leave Leningrad," the officer went on, ignoring Alexi and turning toward Poppa, "you will report to Collective Farm No. 138 in Narkutsk, Comrade Makarovitch. Our generous Soviet government has decided to give you one more chance to change your mind. You will be the lowest worker in rank and pay at Collective Farm No. 138. Perhaps then you will be willing to forget your religion and be a loyal Soviet engineer once more."

"Narkutsk?" Poppa, who sat stunned, finally asked.

Tanya began to weep softly and buried her face in her mother's lap. But the KGB officer ignored the girl.

"You will leave Leningrad, and you will live in Narkutsk. We have checked with the Ministry of Cults and discovered that there is no church in Narkutsk. You will be the only Christians, no doubt, and you had better not try to contaminate others." The police officer walked toward the door.

"Narkutsk? Where is Narkutsk?" Poppa persisted.

"You will find out soon enough," the KGB officer mumbled.

Turning away from the dazed family, the officer brusquely joined his comrade still standing by the apartment door. The other man hurriedly buttoned his long coat as if he were eager to leave.

The officer with the black hat was ready to walk out the door when he abruptly strode instead to a shortwave radio standing on a wooden cabinet. "I suppose you think you will continue to listen to your Christianity on that!" he shouted as he struck the radio with his fist. "Well, in Narkutsk you will be too far away to hear your foreign radio sermons."

The KGB officer lifted the white embroidered cloth which covered the large radio receiver. *"Bibliya!"*

The officer had come to the apartment with such high hopes—so sure that a sensible chat would be enough to change Mr. Makarovitch and his family. Now the black Bible seemed to symbolize the failure of his whole mission.

He snatched the Bible.

"Please, please comrade police officer!" Tanya flung herself from her mother's lap. "That's the Bible God gave us in Czechoslovakia. Please, please . . ." she begged. "God Himself gave that Bible to us—it is a miracle story. He gave it to us through Gregori, the soldier . . ." Tanya started to say.

But Mr. Makarovitch interrupted his daughter. "Tanya, the police officer does not care how we got our Bible. But perhaps he will be kind enough to let us keep our precious Bible."

In reply the officer jerked the Bible from Alexi, who had put his hand on the black cover while Tanya spoke. "I'll throw your Bible in the Neva River!" The police officer shoved the book into his coat pocket, and the two men stomped out the door.

"But, Poppa, our Bible! The Bible that the soldier Gregori gave us . . ." Tanya wailed as the sound of footsteps died away down the cement hall. "We waited so long for a Bible, and now it's gone." Tanya wept.

"Pozhaluysta, dyetki—please, children." Momma struggled to be calm. "We must not cry. We must thank God they did not arrest us. At least Poppa will have a job," she said, trying to cheer her frightened children. "Now we must find out where Narkutsk is," she said bravely, but her voice shook.

"Poppa, I don't want to go to Narkutsk!" Alexi's brown eyes protested. "Leningrad is our home. We have done nothing wrong. It is only because we are believers that they are sending us away. You are not a collective farmer—you are an engineer!"

Poppa smiled sadly at his indignant son who stood so straight and spoke so earnestly. "You are right, Alexi. We have done nothing wrong. But that is not why we are being punished. Our Soviet leaders hate God because they do not know Him. They are punishing us because we are obeying Christ.

"Do you remember, Alexi, what Gregori said when he gave us the Bible in Czechoslovakia?" Poppa asked.

Alexi recalled the soldier's words. "Gregori said he prayed the Bible would help us to be good soldiers too—soldiers of the Cross," Alexi replied, his voice faltering.

Thoughtfully Poppa smiled and began to sing a song that a Christian had written many years earlier in a Siberian prison.

When we finish the fierce battle here on earth,
Soldiers of the cross of Christ,
We will come to our holy, heavenly home . . . .

By the time the family had finished the song, Alexi felt comforted, but still an icicle of fear stabbed tormentingly. *What would Narkutsk be like?*

"Narkutsk . . . Narkutsk." Poppa had pulled a huge map of Russia from the bookcase and was running his finger down the index. Alexi hung over his father's shoulder.

"There, Poppa! I found it!" Alexi exclaimed

18

excitedly. With trembling fingers he traced the map to the family's new home in a line straight east from the Ural Mountains to a city on the Okal River.

"It—it is in Siberia." Poppa struggled to conceal the dismay of his discovery.

"Siberia—oh, it will be so cold, Ivan." Momma pulled the knitted shawl she wore around her shoulders as if she could already feel the freezing Siberian winter. "And so much snow, too." She stroked a leaf of the green *feekoos* plant.

"Sibir!" Tanya leaped from her chair and her long, black braids bounced happily. "Oh, Poppa! I've always wanted to go to Siberia. We've been studying about Siberia in school. There are mountains and trees and wild country. We are going to the frontier. We will be pioneers!" She threw her arms around her father.

Poppa's eyes brightened as he hugged his elated daughter. "Yes, Tanyatchka," he addressed his daughter affectionately, "when God closes one door, He opens another." Poppa smiled. "And who knows, Tanyatchka, where our Siberian adventure will lead us."

2.

Alexi Finds a Friend

"Alexi! Tanya! Wake up!" Mrs. Makarovitch gently shook her sleeping children as the train struggled through the snowy forest. "We are only a few hours from Narkutsk, and the sun is out at last. You better look outside quickly before the sun goes down again," Momma said, smiling. "The mountains are magnificent!"

Alexi rubbed his eyes and uncurled stiffly from his sleep. It was the third night that he, his mother, father, and sister Tanya had slept sitting up in the cramped train compartment. Now there were three other passengers squeezed into the crowded compartment with the Makarovitches.

Alexi sat beside an old *babushka*—grandmother—who snuggled a crate at her feet with two chickens inside. The chickens flapped their wings against the wooden slats of the crate. The babushka held a raveled woolen blanket ready to wrap around the crate when she stepped outside into the freezing air.

The train compartment was warm and cozy, but Alexi shivered as snow from the icy railroad tracks thrashed against the window. Curiously he pressed his forehead against the frosted pane. Except for the gray sky and a few clusters of evergreen trees which had shed their coats of snow, the world outside was white.

White—and mysterious, Alexi mused as he studied the Siberian mountains so different from Leningrad's flat countryside. *Siberia? Narkutsk? What will they really be like? Siberia is such a long way from Leningrad.*

During the three busy days of packing after the police officer had told them they had to leave Leningrad, one terror had tugged relentlessly at Alexi's troubled mind. What would happen at school when the other children discovered why the Makarovitches had moved to Siberia? Would the teachers know Poppa had been exiled to Narkutsk by the police just because he believed in God and told others about Jesus?

By the time the train arrived in Narkutsk that afternoon, the winter sun that stayed so seldom in the sky had already slipped behind the mountains circling the city. Narkutsk stood bleak and cold against the leaden sky.

The first night in Narkutsk, the family slept on benches in the train station. Poppa carefully pushed the suitcases with their few belongings they had carried from Leningrad under the long bench where he slept.

By the second night, the chairman of Collective Farm No. 138 had assigned the Makarovitches an apartment in the northeast section of the city where

Poppa could take a trolley to work at the collective farm on the outskirts of Narkutsk.

One afternoon a few days later, Mrs. Makarovitch and Alexi huddled near the stove in the tiny fifth-floor apartment that looked much like the one they had left in Leningrad—two small rooms plus a kitchen and a bathroom. Like so many buildings in Narkutsk, a young pioneering Siberian town, the gray cement apartment was new—bordered by other buildings still unfinished whose empty windows stared like vacant eyes onto the wide, snowy streets.

"Do we have to go to school right away?" Alexi asked.

"But of course you must go to school!" Momma stoked the fire burning in the black cast-iron stove. "Poppa has already started work at the collective farm, and I must find a job in the factory. We will all be busy.

"It is only February. You must finish the winter semester, Alexi, and soon the spring thaw will come. Then it will be summer, and school will be over for the year," Mrs. Makarovitch said, trying to encourage her son.

"But, Momma, I don't know anyone in Narkutsk. I've never gone to a new school. What will the teacher say when she discovers I am a Christian and don't wear a red scarf?" Fear flooded Alexi's mind.

Tanya entered the apartment from the hall with an armload of laundry which was stiff from hanging in the frozen air outside. She overheard her brother's fears. "Maybe we will get teachers like Meria Petrovna," Tanya added, voicing her own anxieties. "Maybe they will try to make us wear a red scarf and join the Young Pioneers."

"Dyetki—children," Momma intervened, "God has brought us safely to Siberia, and Siberia is not as bad as we feared. God has given us an apartment." She gestured gratefully at the still-barren rooms. "And your father is thankful for his job at the collective farm. God will go before you, too. You will be happy in your new school."

The next day when Alexi and Tanya started to school, the temperature was 30 degrees below zero and the Siberian sun hung low, as if frozen in the sky. Smoke from chimneys and the exhaust from blue and gray buses stayed suspended like clouds in the air. The whole world seemed frozen.

Alexi felt the bitter cold penetrating through his black wool coat, but still he lagged behind—prolonging the moment when he must walk through the gate of school No. 166 and face a new and frightening world. But his mother had said that he must lead the way because Tanya was younger.

When the children finally reached the wall that surrounded the barren school and walked through the foreboding black metal gate, the darkness had not lifted. With a feeling of gloom, Alexi recalled that Siberia had even fewer hours of daylight in winter than Leningrad. By the time the sun rose briefly around noon, he and Tanya would be shut inside the school.

Tanya hung close to her brother. "I wish we could be in the same room, Alexi," she said wistfully, surveying the courtyard full of children shadowed by the tall, gray school.

Alexi did not ignore his sister as he sometimes did. "I—I wish we could stay together too, Tanya," he admitted gently.

Inside the courtyard two boys with hockey sticks slung across their back jostled past Alexi. "Quick, Tanya!" Alexi motioned excitedly to his sister. "Let's see where they're going!" They followed the boys to a shiny building with a sign in Russian that said "Gymnasium."

Alexi wanted to trail the boys inside where he was sure he'd find a hockey rink. But at that moment a bell shrilled in the courtyard. "Tanya, maybe—I think I might like this school!"

"Room 105 for you, Tanya Makarovitch," the principal, a strong, smiling woman, announced. She glanced at Alexi. "And you, Alexi Makarovitch, will be assigned to Room 306—that's Olga Yakovna's room."

Room 306 was already filling with children when Alexi finally found the large classroom. The windows, he discovered, faced the gymnasium. He gazed happily toward the hockey rink and hoped he would soon be included in the games.

Olga Yakovna, a young teacher with blonde hair pulled tightly back from her pretty face into a severe bun on top of her head, sat stiffly in front of the room grading papers under a scowling portrait of Lenin. "So you are the new student—Alexi Ivanovich Makarovitch. Is that correct?" she greeted Alexi unsmilingly.

"Yes, Olga Yakovna," Alexi replied, standing respectfully in front of the teacher's desk.

"First we will fill out your entry form." Olga Yakovna bent to pull an entry form from her desk drawer.

"Name? Last school? How long did you live in Leningrad?" Swiftly Olga Yakovna jotted information on the paper. When the last question was answered, she leaned back and studied her new student. "Only one thing is lacking, Alexi Ivanovich. Where is your badge? You should at least remember to wear it on your first day at school."

"My badge?"

"Yes, your red scarf like all the children wear."

Alexi flushed. "I do not wear the red scarf, Olga Yakovna," he faltered. "I—I do not belong to the Young Pioneers."

"What!" All trace of patience faded from the teacher's face. "How could you *not* belong to the Young Pioneers? Are you not a loyal young communist? Are you not loyal to our leader Lenin?

"From your last school record I see that you have excellent grades—excellent conduct—you are said to be honest." She paused. "Surely you are qualified to join the Young Pioneers."

"I do not belong to the Young Pioneers, Olga Yakovna, because—because I am not an atheist." Suspicion crept into Olga Yakovna's expression. "I am a *verruyuschiy*—I believe in God," Alexi stammered.

"A *verruyuschiy!*" But instead of showing the fury that Alexi expected her to, his teacher sank wearily into her chair. "How can it be?" The teacher seemed bewildered. "Not another one!"

"Are there other Christians here?" Alexi could not conceal the hope in his eyes.

"Do not be encouraged, Alexi Makarovitch," the teacher answered coldly. "Even if there are other Christians, that will make it no easier for you."

Her voice strained in exasperation, she said, "Why can you Christians not understand? All good citizens of our motherland Russia are communists. To be a good communist, Alexi," she continued earnestly, "you cannot be a Christian. Our leader Lenin said himself that religion is an 'opiate of the people.' It numbs the mind. A *relighioznik* cannot be a true soldier of communism," she warned.

"Please, Alexi," she pleaded, "before you bring trouble on yourself, be an obedient boy. Wear the red scarf. Even if you do not tell your parents you belong to the Young Pioneers, just wear the red scarf here at school."

Alexi struggled. He *could* wear the red scarf, he reasoned to himself, only at school. If he wore the red scarf he would belong in Narkutsk. He wouldn't be an outsider like he had always been at his school in Leningrad. And Olga Yakovna was sincere. She *did* say she wanted to help him.

But if he wore the red scarf, Alexi thought as he silently weighed the consequences, then he would have to say he did not believe in God.

Alexi noticed that the other students had started to listen. He tried to speak softly. "It is not just because Momma and Poppa believe in God that I cannot belong, but I believe in God myself, Olga Yakovna."

"You have made your choice," the young teacher said crossly. "My duty as a teacher is to train you to be a loyal young communist. Now I have no choice. I must try to change you." Olga Yakovna waved Alexi to a seat at the rear of the room.

Alexi's cheeks burned as he marched back through the aisle of curious children who had grown silent listening to his conversation with the teacher. He slipped into his desk and stared straight ahead.

But then suddenly he remembered Olga Yakovna's words: "Not another one!" He felt heartened. Maybe there was another Christian—maybe another boy right in his own class! But why had the police officer said there was no church in Narkutsk? Hopes and doubts tugged at Alexi's mind all that day.

It was during the last class of the day, music instruction, when Olga Yakovna announced, "Now, students, we will sing our patriotic song." She held up a large poster with the words, "Lenin is my friend. In joy and in sorrow, he is always with me . . ."

Alexi didn't sing and Olga Yakovna glanced reprovingly in his direction, but it was not Alexi she scolded when she stopped angrily in the middle of the song and faced a student across the room. "Yuri Samkov," she said, frowning, "I notice you are not singing praises to our leader, Lenin. You will come to the front of the room and explain why."

A boy with ruddy cheeks, who looked as if he had just come in out of the snow, walked hesitantly to the front. "I honor our leader, Lenin, Olga Yakovna," he spoke respectfully, "but I—I cannot worship Lenin. I worship God."

"Then you also cannot play in the class hockey game tomorrow night!" Olga Yakovna snapped. She watched with satisfaction as disappointment flickered across the boy's face.

Yuri was a Christian! Alexi's heart beat wildly. There *was* another believer—right in his classroom! Olga Yakovna hadn't wanted to tell him. But now he knew.

29

When school was over, Alexi wanted to rush to Yuri's desk, but he felt Olga Yakovna's suspicious stare as he rose to leave the room. Quickly Alexi darted to the front gate where he had promised to meet Tanya. There was only one gate into the school courtyard. Yuri would have to walk through, so he waited.

Through the gloomy winter afternoon, Alexi saw Yuri caught in a crowd of children shoving through the gate. Alexi elbowed into the group beside him. He had to speak swiftly. "Are you—are you a *verruyuschiy?*" he blurted.

Yuri stared at Alexi in surprise, then suddenly broke into a bright smile, "A *verruyuschiy?* Yes, yes, I am a believer!" he exclaimed happily.

The two boys walked in silence for a few seconds until they were safely past the school gate, and then they both spoke at once.

"You are the new boy . . ."

"You are a Christian!"

"You like hockey too!" Their words tumbled over each other.

"There's a place on the river where we play hockey," Yuri said, pointing eastward past a birch grove.

"The police officer told us there weren't any churches in Narkutsk," Alexi explained when he had finished telling Yuri how his family had come to live in Siberia.

Yuri glanced over his shoulder to see if anyone was listening. His eyes gleamed. "Alexi, we are truly brothers—in Christ. I will tell you a secret." His voice dropped to a whisper. "I will tell you where the Christians meet!"

3.

So Many Bibles!

"Alexi! Where were you?" Tanya exclaimed angrily when she finally spied her brother running back toward the school gate. She stomped her feet to keep warm and rubbed her mittened hands together. "You know I was waiting at the gate," she sniffed. "Besides, Momma said not to run in the winter air. You'll freeze your lungs."

"I'm sorry, Tanya," Alexi admitted, quickly pushing his straight black hair from his eyes, "but wait till you hear what happened!"

Swiftly Alexi told his sister about Yuri. "He's a Christian, and he likes hockey." Enthusiastically Alexi stopped to scoop a snowball from the sidewalk.

"And guess what, Tanya! Yuri told me where the believers meet." Alexi pulled his coat closer to shut out the piercing stabs of cold air in the dark Siberian afternoon. "The government won't let the Christians meet in a church building here, so they have to meet in a house. But the authorities do not allow house meetings . . ."

"But how can there be Christians in Narkutsk?" Tanya was confused. "The police in Leningrad said . . ."

"It's not true, Tanya." Alexi turned toward his sister and almost bumped into a fisherman carrying a huge hunk of ice chopped from the frozen Okal River.

"Watch out, boy," the man grumbled.

Poppa was already home from the collective farm when Alexi bounded through the apartment door, eager to tell his parents the exciting news about Yuri. "He wrote out the address for me," Alexi said, digging deep into his pocket. He handed the slip of paper to his father.

"28 Orloff Street," Poppa read the address aloud. But a troubled frown wrinkled his forehead.

"Alexi, are you sure Yuri is a believer? Perhaps God has answered our prayer through Yuri and shown us the place to find other Christians." Poppa hesitated. "But, on the other hand, we must be careful."

"Poppa! I know Yuri is a believer. Even Olga Yakovna, my teacher, knows he's a Christian. I'm sure Yuri told the truth."

The next night the Makarovitches hurried to get ready for the Christian meeting. "You'd better wear your wool sweater under your heavy coat, Alexi. And Tanya, don't forget to wear two pairs of long stockings," Mrs. Makarovitch cautioned her children when she peeked through the faded lace curtains at the snowy, frozen night outside.

The family stepped off the warm, crowded trolley

several blocks ahead of the address. "So no one will ask questions about where we're going," Alexi whispered to Tanya, who was complaining that her toes would freeze from walking so far.

Snowflakes, larger than any Alexi had ever seen in Leningrad, stuck on his coat as the family stumbled through the dry, drifting snow toward the house church. It was Alexi who found the address first. The number "28" was covered with dirty ice and scratched into the high gate of a wooden fence that circled the house.

"What if this isn't the right house? What if Yuri didn't tell the truth?" Tanya asked, clinging anxiously to her father.

"Of course Yuri told the truth!" Alexi hissed.

Poppa firmly pressed the buzzer on the picket gate and in moments a shriveled old man with a silvery gray beard slowly pried open the gate. Huddled in a long black coat, he peered fearfully at the family standing before him.

"We are *verruyuschiye*—believers," Poppa whispered. "Is this the house where the believers worship?"

"*Verruyuschiye!*" the old man exclaimed as he flung the gate wide to the family. "Welcome, welcome! I am Igor Davidovich Babitsky." He wrung their hands warmly, and his white beard bobbed as he spoke.

"Follow me!" Igor Davidovich said as he led the way into a bright blue cottage with icicles hanging from the carved wood borders that decorated the windowsills and door.

Even though the Makarovitches had come early, the one large room in the cottage was already crowded.

33

"Zhenya, my wife, and I took the walls out to make our house bigger for the meetings. Now our home is a *molitveniy dom*—house of prayer," Igor explained proudly.

At first the Christians glanced apprehensively at the Makarovitches, but then Igor's beaming announcement dispelled their fears. "They are *nahshee*—one of us!" he exclaimed, and from all over the room people came to welcome and embrace the family.

Alexi started across the room to search for Yuri, but an old man with whiskers stooped to hug him. "How did you find our meeting, little brother?" he asked. But before Alexi could answer or continue his search for Yuri, it was time for the meeting to begin.

The preacher stood at the front of the big room and the people waited with expectation as he opened his Bible.

Alexi glanced around the room. To his great astonishment he saw that several of the Christians held black Bibles. And surprisingly, the Bibles all looked the same—no notebooks, no portions of Scripture hand-copied on pieces of paper like the Christians had in Leningrad. Where had the believers found so many Bibles? Alexi was puzzled.

Sadly Alexi thought of the printed Bible the KGB officer had snatched out of his hands in Leningrad only a few weeks before. Alexi's hopes rose as he counted the Bibles sprinkled among the believers. Maybe in Narkutsk God would give his family another Bible.

But then he remembered his father's bleak words only the night before when Tanya had prayed for a Bible. "Not many tourists come to Siberia,

Tanyatchka. We are a long way from anywhere. It may not be so easy to find a Bible here."

The meeting was already half finished when Alexi heard the door at the back of the room creak open. He felt his father, who was standing beside him, stiffen. Instinctively the Christians, who were already standing close together, crowded even closer, until they formed a barrier of protection around the preacher at the front.

"Who could be coming so late?" a young mother, who held a bewildered child by the hand, anxiously asked her husband.

"Oh, Ivan. What if it is the police?" Alexi heard his mother whisper fearfully.

Anxiously Alexi remembered that Yuri had said: "The police or their helpers, the *druzhiniky,* come sometimes to our meetings. Sometimes they just make noise and try to stop the meeting."

But Alexi also knew that at other times the police fined believers who allowed Christian meetings to be held in their homes. Alexi glanced apprehensively toward Igor who owned the blue cottage. But the old man's head was bowed in prayer.

Suddenly out of the tense silence someone shouted joyfully, "It is Aleksandr Sergeyevich! Our Alyosha! He's home!" Happy voices rippled through the crowd and transformed the fear of a few moments before to joy.

Alexi turned to stare at the stranger—a tall, powerful man wearing high boots. His hair was gray and his face looked gaunt and weary, but his piercing blue eyes shone and his joyful smile brightened the whole room of Christians.

The gathered believers rushed to embrace the stranger. "Alyosha, Alyosha is home," an old babushka said, hobbling toward the tall man. "How I wish it were spring and I had some lilacs to give our Alyosha."

"Who is he, Poppa?" Alexi wondered aloud to his father.

"I—I'm not sure, Alexi." Poppa's voice was puzzled. "But he must be someone special."

A man standing nearby overheard Alexi's question. "It is our dear General Aleksandr Sergeyevich— or at least he used to be a general in our Soviet army before he became a Christian five years ago," the man explained. "Then the authorities expelled him from the army. Two years ago they put our dear Aleksandr Sergeyevich in prison."

By now Aleksandr Sergeyevich had reached the front of the room, and the Christians turned solemn and silent again as they waited for the general to speak.

"*Bratya i syostri*—brothers and sisters." The tall man's voice was steady, and his hands were closed firmly around a Bible—the same kind of Bible as the other believers held. "Just today I was released from the prison. I came straight from prison to you," he reported joyfully.

Alexi leaned forward. There was something compelling in the way the general spoke—something gripping in the glint of his penetrating eyes.

"It is five years since I first walked in the way of Christ," the general said. "Five years since I heard the Gospel broadcasts for the first time in this city and became a follower of Christ. Thank God for the brothers and sisters outside who haven't forgotten us.

Slava Bogu—thank God for the radio broadcasts," he said fervently.

"Broadcasts?" Alexi wondered if he had heard right. He remembered clearly the night the police had told his family they must leave Leningrad. "You'll never hear the Christian radio broadcasts in Siberia," the secret police officer had sneered.

"You all know my life before I became a Christian, brothers and sisters," the general continued. "I myself knew our leader Lenin. As a young soldier I fought for Lenin. All my life I have defended our country." The general straightened proudly.

"Once my chest was decorated with medals for bravery," he continued, glancing at his gray prisoner's shirt which had replaced a uniform covered with shining medals.

"Is he a real general?" Alexi whispered in amazement to his father.

"Although I was a good general in our Soviet army," Aleksandr Sergeyevich said, sighing softly as if he had overheard Alexi's question, "I did not know God. Now, brothers and sisters." He leaned toward the crowd before him. "I am still a loyal citizen of our motherland Russia, but I am also a soldier of Christ." The general's eyes glinted like a sword as he spoke.

Alexi longed to meet the general. "Maybe I could ask him where to find the Christian radio broadcasts," he said softly. But he suddenly felt shy. He was not sure he had courage to speak to a real army *gehnyeral!*

After the meeting so many people crowded around the former army officer that Alexi could not even squeeze close. He turned instead to search for Yuri. "I—I've never talked to the general either—I wish I could," Yuri admitted wistfully when the two boys finally found each other.

Alexi was about to ask Yuri if it were possible to hear the Christian broadcasts in Siberia when he overheard his father ask one of the preachers the same question.

"We seldom hear the missionary radio station from Europe here in Siberia," the preacher explained, "but there are two other stations located in Korea and in the Philippine Islands. Their signals come into Narkutsk loud and clear."

That night Alexi tossed fitfully on his narrow bed that the family used as a couch during the day. His sister Tanya slept in a small bed across the room, and he heard his father's steady snore from the bedroom.

It had been a good day. In Narkutsk he had Yuri for a friend. In Leningrad he had never had a Christian friend in the same class at school. Alexi missed the Christians his family had known so well in Leningrad. But there were Christians in Narkutsk—Christians who met in a house. Suddenly Alexi realized he no longer felt afraid of Siberia. Siberia was not so different from Leningrad.

However, questions filled his mind. How could he meet the strong, kind general? And what about the Bible the general had held in his hands? The general wasn't the only one who had a Bible. Many of the Christians had Bibles. And the Bibles all looked the same. There was something mysterious . . .

4.

Alexi Faces a Decision

The next day Alexi exchanged glances with Yuri across the classroom. He waited for a safe moment to speak to his friend away from Olga Yakovna's suspicious stare.

When the boys hurried to hockey class through the long hall that linked the school to the gymnasium, Alexi questioned his friend. "Last night at the meeting—so many of the Christians had Bibles—even the general."

Alexi spoke softly as he told Yuri about the Bible his family once owned that a soldier gave them in Czechoslovakia. Yuri's eyes were sympathetic when Alexi explained, "It was the first Bible we ever had, but the secret police—when they came to our apartment to tell us to leave Leningrad—they took our Bible."

Yuri and Alexi hung back as the other boys pushed past them into the gym. When they were alone, Alexi

39

asked, "Is it possible to buy Bibles in Narkutsk—*in Siberia?*"

Yuri answered carefully, "I think I could help your family find a Bible, Alexi," he said, "but I can't tell you here. Later—after school."

On the hockey rink, Alexi played with all his might—every thought pushed from his mind except the wild desire to drive the puck into the net. Again and again he passed the puck across the ice to Yuri. Together they skillfully maneuvered the puck past the players on the other team.

By the time the fast-moving game was over, Alexi was exhausted. But he was also exhilarated. "Three goals!" the other players exclaimed with admiration. "Alexi Makarovitch scored three goals!"

After the game, Coach Pavel Akimovich Lubarov, a sturdy man with thick sandy hair who wore a bright blue sportsman's uniform, beckoned Alexi to a corner of the rink.

"Alexi Makarovitch," he said to Alexi as if he were addressing an adult, "I liked what I saw out on the rink today. You know how to handle that stick!"

Alexi's cheeks crimsoned with pleasure at the compliment. Such praise, and from the coach himself!

"Perhaps you know our team is in the championship playoffs for Sotkin District this year," the coach continued, studying Alexi's response. "Have you considered trying out for the school team, Alexi?"

"Yes, yes, Pavel Akimovich," Alexi admitted to the coach. "But we were sent—we moved to Narkutsk too late for me to try out," he stammered.

"I see." The coach paced the floor at the side of the rink. "Listen, Alexi," he said, putting his hand on

Alexi's shoulder, "last night Pyotr Borisovich was injured."

"But isn't he on the championship team?" Alexi asked. He thought he had remembered Yuri mentioning Pyotr's name when they talked about the hockey team.

"That's right." The coach looked steadily at Alexi. "Alexi, do you think you could step in and take Pyotr's place? There's only one more week before the first game of the championship playoffs begins. It's not much time to get acquainted with the team's style, but I think you're the right player to substitute for Pyotr Borisovich."

Alexi felt as if he would smother from so much happiness. He had always hoped to play on a real hockey team. Now Pavel Akimovich was asking him—the new boy—to join the coach's championship team!

"Yes, yes!" Alexi replied quickly, as if he were afraid the coach might change his mind. "Thank you, Pavel Akimovich! I will do my best for our team," he said as proudly as if he were already a team member.

"There's just one more thing," the coach said, taking his hand from Alexi's shoulder. "I know you are not a member of the Young Pioneers, Alexi. Usually a team member must belong. However, in this emergency I think we could make an exception.

"But I have heard rumors." The coach hesitated. "You aren't a *verruyuschiy*—a believer—are you, Alexi?"

Alexi felt as if a mountain had fallen upon him. The boys from the locker room swarmed back by the rink on their way to classes—their blue uniforms a blur before him. "I do know of the Christians," Alexi began.

"Well, if that is all," the coach said, obviously relieved. He slapped Alexi encouragingly on the back. "That is all I need to know. It is all right to *know* of the Christians. Just so you are not one of them!" The coach strode off toward the locker room.

Dazed, Alexi turned. Yuri had come from the locker room and stood silently by his side. Shame tore at Alexi. Had his friend overheard? Then Alexi saw the hurt in Yuri's eyes. Yuri knew!

"I'll wait while you change, and we can walk home from school," Yuri offered, but the familiar warmth had vanished from his voice. Unable to face his friend a moment longer, Alexi fled toward the locker room.

Only a few minutes before, Alexi felt as if he had conquered the world. Now he felt like a coward. He had betrayed Yuri. A terrible realization rose in him. Not only had he betrayed Yuri, he had betrayed Momma, Poppa, the other Christians. He had even denied Christ Himself.

Alexi hoped Yuri wouldn't wait. But when he returned from the locker room, Yuri was listlessly leaning on his white and red hockey stick.

Yesterday on the walk home, when the boys were away from Olga Yakovna's stern classroom, they had talked, laughed, thrown snowballs, and there was seldom a second of silence.

Tonight as they crunched through the snow, Yuri said nothing about Alexi's conversation with the coach. Alexi struggled to speak but kept his eyes on the snowy sidewalk. The snow, he noticed, was studded with specks of dirt from a nearby factory.

"About the Bibles—you were going to tell me about the Bibles," Alexi said finally when they had marched several steps in silence and were almost to the Makarovitches' apartment door.

"I—I'm sorry, Alexi. I can't tell you now. I had plans for us, but . . ." Yuri turned and fled.

Dismally Alexi pushed open the heavy metal door that led into the apartment building. He trudged dejectedly up the five flights of stairs to the apartment.

"Alexi!" Mrs. Makarovitch hugged her son. She helped him as he struggled to take off his heavy wool coat, scarf, and knitted cap. "Didn't you have hockey today?" His mother's blonde hair shone softly in the dim lamplight, and her face was sympathetic.

"You look so sad. Come—sit in the kitchen while I finish fixing the borscht. Have a *bulochka,* bun, and tell me about today," she urged. Alexi followed her toward the kitchen which was steaming with the delicious beet soup.

Alexi picked up the *bulochka* but he didn't feel hungry. "No, I can't tell you, Momma," he murmured and wished he were out in the snowy street— anywhere—just so he could be by himself. Then maybe his shame would seem less suffocating.

"Well, Alexi, we will talk later." Momma spooned more beets into the borscht. "But now I have some news for you—some good news! Guess who is coming to supper tonight?" Momma smiled—happy to share her surprise. "Somebody you want very much to meet," she hinted.

"Not the general!" Alexi gasped.

"But, Alexi." Momma was mystified. "You look frightened. What happened to you today?"

Before Momma could ask another question, a firm knock sounded on the apartment door. "The general," she said. "He said he was coming early." She took off her apron and turned eagerly toward the door.

In agony Alexi rose from the chair. He must greet the general and be polite. But how could he look into the general's eyes—those penetrating blue eyes that revealed such depth of Christian devotion and honesty?

"And you must be Alexi," the general said, pulling his chair close to Alexi. "You know, my parents called me Alyosha when I was a boy."

"Yes, Aleksandr Sergeyevich." Alexi felt his face flush as he looked down at the floor.

"Alexi has just come from hockey class," Mrs. Makarovitch said, smiling proudly at her son. She set glasses of hot tea in metal holders before the general and Alexi. Alexi stared at the shiny tea holders his mother used only when guests came. One was painted gold with scenes from the victory of Volgograd engraved on it.

"Ah, hockey—I used to like to play myself." The general smiled. "And who is your hockey coach, Alexi?"

"It is Pavel Akimovich Lubarov," Alexi replied, feeling embarrassed that he could think of nothing more to say.

"Ah, Pavel Akimovich," the general said warmly. "I know him well. He also grew up in Narkutsk. When I was still in the army, he was a soldier under my command—a good soldier with a kind heart.

"I tell you, Alexi." The general leaned across the table toward Alexi. "I have thought often of Pavel

45

Lubarov, but I have not seen him since I became a Christian. Even when I was in prison, I thought, 'When I am free, I must go visit Pavel Akimovich and tell him about Christ.' "

"Yes, Aleksandr Sergeyevich," Alexi said weakly, and the whole flood of all that had happened that afternoon in hockey class swept miserably over him again.

Later, when the family sat around the table eating borscht, *bulochki,* and thin slices of fish and reindeer meat, Poppa asked the general a question. "Aleksandr Sergeyevich," he said, his voice very earnest, "at the meeting last night we noticed many Bibles. But Bibles—in Siberia?" Poppa was perplexed.

The general hunched forward as if he were afraid someone might overhear his conversation. "My little brother and sister," he said, turning toward Alexi and Tanya, "you must not repeat what I will tell you this night."

The general relaxed slightly but still spoke softly. "As you know, there is not one Bible for sale in any bookstore in our whole country." He gestured in a helpless circle with his large hands. "Many believers would give a month's wages for a Bible if they could only find one to buy.

"Our people are starving to read God's Word. Four years ago, some Christians here in Siberia traveled to visit our government officials in Moscow and asked, 'Since you will not print Bibles for us, may we have permission according to our Soviet constitution to print Bibles ourselves?'"

"What did the leaders say?" Alexi asked, absorbed in the story. Momentarily he forgot his own troubles.

"Some of the leaders were thrown into prison," the general replied gravely. "Others were fined and told to return to Siberia and stop causing trouble.

"After the Christians had tried in every way to receive official permission from the government to print Bibles," the general continued, "they decided they must have God's Word—at any cost.

"Now some Christians here in Siberia have built a secret press." The general paused and glanced around the room as if he were afraid the walls could hear. "These believers are printing Bibles for the rest of us. I cannot tell you more," the general said sadly, "but we must pray for these brave brothers and sisters. They are soldiers of Christ." He spoke with admiration.

"Printing Bibles! And on a secret press!" Slowly the danger dawned on Alexi. "Have any of the Christians been caught printing Bibles, Aleksandr Sergeyevich?" he asked.

The general's eyes showed suffering. "Three years ago, young brother, I was delivering Bibles printed on the secret press to some Christians in another city in Siberia who had no *dukhovnovo khleba*—no spiritual bread.

"That night the police checked all luggage on the train. They opened my suitcase and found the Bibles." Alexi leaned tensely toward the general. "For many days the secret police tried to force me to tell them who had given me the Bibles," the general said. "They wanted me to lead them to the secret press. They wanted me to deny I was a Christian. By God's help I refused. Then I was sentenced to prison."

That night before the general left the apartment, he reached into the pocket of his heavy wool overcoat and handed a black book to Alexi's father. *"Bibliya*—from the secret press for your family," he smiled.

"The Bible—is it truly for us?" Poppa hesitated and seemed unable to accept such a valuable gift.

Tanya stood on tiptoe to caress the cover of the precious book her father held.

"Slava Bogu—thank God! It is a miracle," Momma wept softly.

Alexi felt no better when before bedtime his father reverently opened the new Bible to the Book of Daniel. Poppa read the story of the three Hebrew youths.

"If we are thrown into the flaming furnace, our God is able to deliver us," the three Hebrew youths told the king who wanted them to bow before the golden idol and deny God.

Long after the general had gone from the little apartment, Alexi lay in sleepless torment. Lifting his eyes to the twisted ice patterns on the window, he knew he had to make a decision.

5.

Poppa's Mysterious Suitcase

By the next morning Alexi had decided. He would go directly to the coach and tell him the truth. "I not only *know* the Christians—I *am* a Christian," he planned to say.

Of course the coach would be furious—just as Olga Yakovna had been that first day at school. Pavel Akimovich had trusted him to help pull the team to victory in the championship playoffs. Now the coach would never trust him again. Miserably Alexi pictured the scene he was sure would follow when he faced the coach.

But as the time for hockey practice approached, a strange, strong peace surrounded his fears. He knew God wanted him to tell the truth.

Across the classroom, Alexi's glance met Yuri, but Yuri quickly bent to the page of arithmetic problems on the desk before him.

That morning on the way to art class, Alexi stopped at his locker for watercolors and drawing paper. A cluster of boys from his class hovered around the lockers—so engrossed in their conversation they did not notice Alexi approach. But he heard them clearly as he bent over into his locker.

"The coach asked Makarovitch to play on the championship team!" one of them exclaimed.

"But isn't Alexi Makarovitch a Christian?" Another boy was bewildered.

"*Da, da*—yes, yes. That is what he told Olga Yakovna," the first boy answered. "But when the coach asked Alexi if he was a *verruyuschiy*, Alexi said he wasn't."

"If I had a chance to play on the championship team, I guess I'd say almost anything," somebody said, and all the boys laughed.

The boy who seemed to be the leader spoke again: "Did you know the coach asked Yuri to substitute on the team before he asked Alexi? But Yuri admitted he was a Christian!" the boy sputtered.

"He's a fool! He's crazy!" the indignant voices exclaimed together.

Finally the boys drifted down the hall, and Alexi turned away from the locker. His face was hot with shame.

So the coach had asked Yuri first. But Yuri told the truth. And the whole school knows I lied, Alexi thought.

"Alexi," the coach welcomed his new team member, "you're early for practice. That's the enthusiastic spirit I like to see! *Ochen khorosho*—good, very good!"

"I am not sure you will want me to stay for practice,

Pavel Akimovich," Alexi said. He wished he could dart back out the door, but he dug his hockey stick into the floor before him and spoke with determination.

"You see, Pavel Akimovich," he continued, "yesterday I did not tell you the whole truth. I do know the Christians, but I am also a Christian myself—a follower of Jesus Christ," he said swiftly, expecting Pavel Akimovich to explode at any moment in a storm of fury.

But a strange expression, almost of admiration, flickered in the coach's eyes. For several seconds, the coach sat silent, studying the boy before him.

"Well, Alexi, you have made your decision. I am sorry. In the future I am afraid that life may not be easy for you." The coach glanced sympathetically at Alexi and strode toward the hockey rink.

With a new freedom, Alexi dashed out of the gymnasium down the snowy street—past a row of slanting wooden houses—past a street of tall, soaring new apartments—past a team of reindeer which looked as if they were laughing while they trotted down the street. The cold Siberian air stung, but Alexi didn't stop. He wanted to be home.

Inside the apartment, fire crackled in the black iron stove and Alexi knew his mother was already home from work at the factory. She stood in the warm kitchen slicing cabbage, sausage, and black bread for supper.

"Alexi, you look so happy! You are a different boy!" she exclaimed gladly.

"I *feel* different, Momma." He grabbed a *bulochka* from inside the cupboard and bit hungrily into the delicious bun.

"And I see you have recovered your appetite." Momma smiled.

Suddenly Alexi felt as if he wanted to tell somebody the whole story. "Momma, yesterday the coach asked me to play on the championship team . . ."

Slowly Alexi related his experience to his mother. She wiped her hands on her apron and sat down at the table to concentrate on her son's story.

"I'm proud of you, Alexi," she said softly when the boy told her about his conversation that day with the coach. She squeezed his hand, "And Alexi—God is pleased."

That night at supper Alexi didn't want to talk about the incident at school. He planned to tell Poppa sometime, but not in front of Tanya.

However, it was Tanya who mentioned the subject.

"Alexi, the whole school is talking about what you told the coach," she said almost shyly.

"Ah! What is the exciting news?" Poppa asked, turning with interest to Alexi.

"It is nothing, Poppa." Alexi frowned at Tanya. "Yesterday . . . well, I made a mistake," Alexi admitted.

"But, Alexi, I am talking about what you told the coach today." Tanya's voice was filled with admiration. "Already the whole school knows you told the coach you could not play in the championships because you are a Christian and cannot join the Young Pioneers."

"Today you have proved yourself to be a true follower of the way of Jesus," Poppa said. His eyes shone as Alexi repeated the whole story.

That night after the family prayed together, they sang the song written by a Siberian Christian in prison.

Poppa smiled proudly at Alexi when they sang the second verse:

> People said about me,
> In battle he will never stand true.
> But they did not know,
> God is my protector and defender.

But one worry still nagged at Alexi: What about Yuri? Would he believe Alexi had really changed? "Will Yuri *ever* trust me again?" Alexi fretted.

The next morning Yuri was waiting in front of the apartment building. He fell in step with Alexi. "I heard what you told the coach yesterday," Yuri said simply, the same friendliness as before in his voice.

"But Yuri . . ." Somehow Alexi felt he must apologize to his friend. "I heard the boys talking by the locker. They said the coach asked you first."

"So now Pavel Akimovich knows there are two Christians in his class," Yuri replied. He grinned and flung a snowball at a birch tree. "Come on, Alexi. I'll race you to the gate!"

The deep snow that had piled high like white blankets tucking in the city when the Makarovitches arrived in February seemed as if it would stay all year around. Even in Leningrad, a city of the north, Alexi had never been as cold. The nights had never seemed so long and the days so dark as they did in Siberia.

But as the weeks turned toward May, the snow slowly faded on the mountains that rimmed the city. The sun climbed steadily higher in the sky until the days grew long and the nights short.

In early May the thick ice on the Okal River broke with a thunderous explosion. Where Alexi and Yuri had played ice hockey only a month before, the ice suddenly tore away. The river thudded ice chunks against its banks, and then rose in torrents as the ice melted and raced downstream.

By the end of May, patches of rich Siberian earth peeked out in sunny spots around the city. Eventually the snow disappeared. The *taiga*—the forested countryside—slowly turned spring green, and Siberia seemed beautiful.

"Let's hunt mushrooms behind the birch grove tonight," Alexi suggested to Yuri on a sunny day as the boys wound their way home from school. "The sun will be up late tonight."

"I wish I could, but . . ." Yuri stopped to search for words. "Well, I have an errand tonight. I have to help somebody," he said vaguely.

Alexi considered Yuri his best friend, but he also sensed that Yuri was concealing something from him—something important. Several times recently Yuri had had mysterious "work" to do. Yuri tried to avoid the subject, but Alexi felt hurt. Why couldn't Yuri tell him? Did Yuri still not trust him completely?

But pride prevented Alexi from questioning his friend further.

That night after the family had listened to the Christian radio broadcast from Korea and read from the Bible the general had given them, Poppa put on his coat. He buttoned it slowly, as if he wished he did not have to leave. "I have a meeting tonight, children," he said. "Don't wait up for me, Galya." He smiled at his wife. "I may be late again."

"Why does Poppa go so often to the meetings?" Tanya asked, looking up from her homework when her

54

father had gone. "Poppa never went to so many meetings in Leningrad."

"Well, there are always meetings that the collective farm workers must attend," Momma said, evading Tanya's questions. "And, of course, your father has many responsibilities among the believers."

Late that night, in a light sleep, Alexi heard the apartment door creak open slowly. Poppa tiptoed quietly into the apartment that was still dimly lighted by the spring sun. Alexi stirred and his father waited by the door, hoping his son would fall asleep again.

But Alexi did not sleep. When his father passed his bed he was awake and saw clearly a big black suitcase in his father's hands.

A suitcase! Alexi was sure his father had carried nothing with him when he left the apartment earlier. Where had his father been? What was he doing? Why was he so late? What was inside the black suitcase?

Why was everyone acting so mysteriously?

6.

The Printing Press

The next night shortly after supper, Poppa reached for his coat. "Well, it looks like another meeting tonight," he announced almost apologetically.

Alexi wanted to ask his father where he was going and why he had returned so late the night before, but the anxiety in his father's eyes made him hesitate.

"I'm glad it is almost June," Mrs. Makarovitch observed. "At least the weather will soon be warmer." She tried to speak cheerfully, but Alexi noticed that she followed his father to the door with a look of concern.

Poppa was still not home when Alexi finished his last homework assignment and crawled into bed.

"Tanya," he whispered to his sister who was lying on her bed across the room, "are you asleep yet?"

"Not yet." Tanya sat up drowsily in her bed. "I hoped Poppa would come home before I fell asleep."

"Tanya, something is wrong," Alexi whispered. "Night after night Poppa goes to meetings. But have you noticed? He seems afraid to tell us where he goes."

Tanya shook her head, "I wish he wouldn't go, Alexi. I'm afraid."

Alexi sat up in bed. "Last night I was awake when Poppa came home. He was carrying a big suitcase. He didn't want me to see it."

"A suitcase! He didn't have a suitcase when he left the apartment," Tanya noted with a puzzled expression.

"That's just it!" Alexi exclaimed. "It's a mystery, but I think I know the answer." He glanced at the bedroom and lowered his voice, careful not to awaken his mother.

"I think Poppa is helping to print Bibles on the secret press. That's why he goes away at night. Momma knows, but they are afraid to tell us because they think we are too young." Alexi forgot to whisper in his excitement at solving the mystery.

"Oh, Alexi!" Tanya gasped. "Poppa could be put in prison—just like the general was." Tanya's voice sounded close to crying.

"Sh! Sh, quiet," Alexi whispered. "Tanya, we can't tell Momma and Poppa that we know," he warned. "Besides, we could be wrong."

The next night when Poppa reached for his coat on the hook by the apartment door, Alexi's questioning glance met his father's eyes.

"Do you have to go to a meeting again tonight, Poppa?" Alexi held back the other questions he wished he dared ask his father. Tanya dropped her study book and waited for her father's answer. Momma sat beside the table unraveling a pair of old mittens. She kept her eyes on her work as she wound the old yarn back into a ball to use again. She would knit new mittens for next winter.

"Yes, children, I must go again tonight," Poppa said wearily. But then, with sudden resolution, he shook his arm out of the coat sleeve and hung the coat back on the hook.

Momma glanced questioningly at Poppa. "I am going to tell the children, Galya," he said decisively. "It is no use to wait any longer. Alexi is almost 13. They are old enough to understand, and they are *verruyuschiye*."

Poppa spoke softly. "You know the Bible the general gave us," he began his explanation. "You remember how happy we felt to have God's Word again. Well, there are thousands of other Christians in Russia who are not as fortunate," Poppa said sadly.

"Poppa—are you helping to print Bibles?" Tanya could contain her curiosity no longer.

"So you already had guessed." Poppa smiled at the children. "It is not that Momma and I didn't trust you, but you are so young. We wanted to protect you. Already you are old beyond your years. You children should be carefree and not struggle with the worries of adults." Poppa sighed. "But in Russia, Christian children must grow up quickly."

"I—we," Alexi carefully included his sister, "Tanya and I promise not to tell. You can trust us."

"Your mother and I knew we could trust you, Alexi. We were sure on the day when you told us what happened at school—when you told the hockey coach about your faith in Jesus."

"But you are still just children," Momma sighed deeply. "Now you must carry the knowledge of adults. You must share the suffering of the other Christians.

"And you must never reveal anything you know about the printing—who is involved, where it is done, how it is done," Poppa cautioned. "Among all the Christians we have agreed to say as little as possible. It is God's work. God will protect the press and the Christians who print the Bibles."

"Do you help print the Bibles?" Tanya's eyes widened as she realized the significance of all her father had said.

"After the Bibles are printed, they are taken to a house to be bound. I go at night to help bind the pages and covers together. Sometimes I bring the Bibles here to pass on to the other Christians."

"So that was what was in the suitcase!" Alexi exclaimed.

"So you knew," Poppa said again. "But now this knowledge must never pass beyond ourselves."

Poppa turned toward the door but then he hesitated. He kneeled beside a chair that stood nearby. "Before I go, let's pray together," he said. "We will pray that people all over Russia will someday be able to read God's holy Word freely." Mr. Makarovitch bowed his head and committed the project to God. And then he was gone into the night.

"Where does Poppa go to sew the bindings on the Bibles?" Alexi asked his mother after his father left.

"To the Samkovs—to the house of Yuri's parents," Momma replied, bending over the yarn she held.

"Yuri's house!" Alexi exclaimed, "So *that* was Yuri's secret!"

"Yes," Momma admitted, "Yuri knows. Sometimes he helps with the work. And Yuri wanted to tell you, Alexi, but Poppa asked him to wait. Your father wanted to tell you and Tanya himself—at the right time."

"Oh, Momma!" Alexi flung his science book aside. "I wish I could go with Poppa. I wish I could help sew bindings on the Bibles!" He paced the floor in frustration.

"Not yet." Momma placed the old yarn on the table. "It is enough for now that you and Tanya guard the secret. Too soon the day will come when you must help," she said soberly. "For now you must say nothing, but you must pray—with patience."

The next day Yuri waited faithfully beside the school gate. "Follow me!" he whispered when he saw Alexi. Hastily Yuri motioned his friend beyond earshot of the school.

"Last night when your father came to my house, he told me you knew the secret," Yuri whispered happily. "Now we are friends in everything, Alexi. I know we must never speak of it—but we can pray."

Later that morning inside the school, Olga Yakovna stood stiffly in front of her class to make an announcement. "Next Monday is a special day of honor for the workers of our city," she told the eager students who sat before her like *matrushka* dolls—some tall, some short. Almost all wore the same kind of uniform—a white blouse and a red scarf tied in a special knot at the neck.

"Yes, yes, it will be a holiday for you also," she promised the hopeful students. "There will be a parade through town and afterward a picnic. Our class will

61

march together in the parade. That is, all of you who belong to the Young Pioneers will march." She glanced at Yuri and then at Alexi.

"All loyal young sons and daughters of Lenin will march in the parade," she said, resuming her explanation. "I am sorry, Yuri Samkov and Alexi Makarovitch, but you have chosen to be disloyal. It is a disgrace to have two students who refuse to wear the red scarf! Do you understand, Yuri Samkov?" She glowered at Yuri who sat in the front row.

"Yes, Olga Yakovna," Yuri mumbled. "I am sorry, Olga Yakovna." But at recess Alexi saw immediately that his friend was not disappointed to miss the parade and picnic.

"Don't you see, Alexi?" Yuri struggled to conceal his excitement in the school yard. "If there's a holiday on Monday, maybe the *molodyosh*—young people from our house church—will organize a meeting in the mountains.

"Last year the *molodyosh* had a youth meeting on Belovat Mountain during the worker's holiday and the weekend before. But I was only 12 then, and the pastors said I was too young to go."

"But now we're both 13!" Alexi interrupted. He was becoming as excited as his friend. "Will we camp in the mountains? Will all the young people go?"

The boys wandered to a corner of the courtyard to discuss the unbelievable prospect—a real youth meeting. "And maybe some of our friends will come from other towns," Yuri speculated hopefully.

That evening Alexi asked his father for permission to attend the youth meeting. "Of course you can go, Alexi," Poppa gladly agreed.

Two days later Yuri stopped by the apartment to give Alexi the final details. "The meeting will start the Saturday before the worker's holiday," he announced eagerly.

"You will meet many other Christian *molodyosh*," Momma said, obviously pleased.

"I wish I were 13 so I could go," Tanya sighed wistfully.

But the next night, Poppa was somber as Alexi prepared to meet the *molodyosh* in the mountains.

"There will be more than just a youth meeting, Alexi," Poppa confided. "A secret mission must be carried out on Belovat Mountain. The general wants to know if you will help."

7.

Secret Mission
on Belovat Mountain

"A secret mission?" Alexi was not sure he had really heard his father correctly.

"Yes, a secret mission," Poppa repeated quietly. He turned on the shortwave radio to drown out their conversation in case it should carry through the thin wall to the apartment next door.

"The general has also invited young people from Komsk to attend the youth meeting on Belovat Mountain," Poppa began.

"Where's Komsk?" Alexi questioned.

"It's the nearest town where other Christians meet—about 100 miles from here. The young people will come on the bus from Komsk to Narkutsk and then hike up to meet you on Belovat Mountain.

"Six months ago the Christians in Komsk were meeting in a house," Poppa continued. "In the middle of the meeting, the police broke into the house and seized the few Bibles the believers had."

"Yuri and I—we could carry Bibles up Belovat Mountain to give to the young people from Komsk," Alexi volunteered, his eyes alight with the exciting plan.

"It seems you understand before I even ask these days. It must be because you are 13, Alexi." For a moment Poppa's eyes were merry.

"The general himself volunteered to deliver Bibles to the believers in Komsk," Poppa picked up his explanation. "But Aleksandr Sergeyevich was only recently released from prison—for delivering Bibles. Now the police are following him again."

"Yuri and I could carry Bibles in our backpacks up the mountain and give them to the *molodyosh* from Komsk," Alexi repeated. He was sure it would work.

Momma stood by the green *feekoos* plant. It was not as tall as the plant she had grown in Leningrad, but the plant was strong, green, and reaching higher every day.

"But he is so young, Ivan," she said as she turned trembling to her husband. "He is still only a boy."

"There is no other way, Galya." Poppa slipped his arm around Momma's shoulder. "If we older Christians carry the Bibles to the youth meeting in the mountains, the authorities will accuse us and say adults have organized a religious youth meeting. The young people must go alone.

"There are at least 20 young people in the church," Poppa planned aloud. "If each of them carries two Bibles to the mountain meeting, that will be safest. That will also mean *dukhovnovo khleba*—much spiritual bread for the believers in Komsk."

66

That night Alexi was far too excited to sleep. Despite his mother's fears, he did not feel frightened. He only felt sorry for the Christians in Komsk whose Bibles had been taken by the police. The boy was sure he should help them.

He remembered how he had felt in Leningrad when the police had torn the Bible from his hands. Then he recalled his family's joy on the night the general had given them a Bible from the secret press.

And Poppa had said there were "at least 20" young people going from Narkutsk. He wondered how many would come from Komsk—Christian young people he had never met before. Like waves, each new excitement of the meeting in the mountains swept over him as he tossed on the narrow bed.

Alexi was still awake when his father opened the apartment door and crept past his bed with the familiar suitcase in his hand. Alexi knew his father had been to the homes of the Christian young people—delivering Bibles for them to carry the next day up the mountain. Alexi turned over and soon he was peacefully asleep.

The day of the mountain retreat dawned clear and cold.

"Don't forget to take your winter coat. It is only June and this is Siberia—not Leningrad," Momma fretted as she wrapped bread, cheese, and sausage in a newspaper bundle for Alexi to stuff in his backpack. At the bottom of the pack, Poppa had placed two black Bibles.

The next morning the streets were thronged with people preparing for the worker's day parade. *Babushkas* busily swept the already tidy streets with hand-tied twig brooms. A band of Komsomol teenagers hung red streamers from all the lampposts.

And a delegation from a tractor factory solemnly nailed huge banners across Narkutsk's main boulevard. "Glory to our great leader, Lenin," one banner proclaimed. "The name and deeds of Lenin will live forever," another sign said.

The trail to Belovat Mountain lay an hour beyond the edge of the city. Alexi and Yuri rode a blue bus to the end of its route in the city. Then they hiked happily through the birch forest that led to the trail up Belovat Mountain.

The trail was not crowded. Most of Narkutsk's citizens were expected to stay in the city to prepare for the parade. However, a short distance up the trail, Alexi and Yuri passed two of the older boys from the Christian house meeting in Narkutsk. But they did not stop to speak. "Don't stop to visit until you are safely on top of the mountain in camp," Poppa had suggested.

As the trail turned toward the top, the trees became sparse and spindly. However, the campground itself was tucked in a clearing shielded by a thicket of trees.

"Alexi Ivanovich—Yuri Petrovich." Swiftly the boys were welcomed into the circle of campers who had already arrived. "Have you met Anatole Vadimich? Lev Maximovich? Anatole plays on the hockey team from Manilov region . . ."

An hour later the older boys decided it was time to set up camp. The girls cut black bread on a stump while the older boys began to pound stakes for a tent. Alexi, Yuri, and two of the younger boys from Komsk set off to gather wood for a campfire.

"Did you bring the Bibles?" one of the boys from

Komsk whispered to Alexi as they bent to the ground gathering sticks.

"Yes," Alexi answered.

"I forgot we're in the forest—safe in the forest," the boy said, laughing. He forgot his fear and spoke out loud.

The meeting began after supper and lasted most of the night. Two boys from Komsk had each carried a *balalaika*—a musical instrument like a guitar—up the mountain. For hours the young people sang— many of the songs were ones they had written themselves.

A girl from Komsk recited a long poem. By the flickering light of the campfire an older boy from Narkutsk read the Book of Daniel aloud. He paused at the story of the Hebrew youths. "There are many kinds of fiery furnaces," he said thoughtfully, "but God will walk with us through them all."

Alexi taught the others several verses of the song his father loved to sing—the one that had been written by a Siberian Christian in prison:

> When we finish the fierce battle here on earth,
> Soldiers of the cross of Christ,
> We will come to our holy, heavenly home . . . .

A circle of stately birch trees stood like sentries with many eyes guarding the gathering of young people forbidden to meet freely in their own country. And the young Christians, who so seldom felt safe if they met in the city, talked, sang, discussed Scripture, and worshiped God with the exhilaration of rare freedom.

At nine o'clock the next night, Sunday, the Siberian

sun still hung over the horizon. The young people were pulling logs around the campfire to make benches for another meeting when they heard footsteps on the trail below.

Before they could guess who was coming to visit their camp, two policemen with red bands on their caps and jackets burst into the forest clearing. The militia medals glinted in the setting sun.

"Do you have a permit to use this campground?" the policeman with the most medals on his uniform asked sternly. "And what youth organization do you represent?" he demanded.

Andrei, a lanky 18-year-old, stepped forward as spokesman. He held out a piece of paper for the policeman to examine. "This is our permit to use the campground and build a campfire," he said.

"You are a *Komsomol*—communist youth—club, I suppose," the policeman who seemed to be the chief said sarcastically.

"No, we are just friends—friends of each other and followers of Jesus," Andrei said straightforwardly.

"Ah—so you admit, it, do you?" the police chief was angry but obviously relieved that his investigation was progressing so swiftly. He pulled a large handkerchief from his pocket and blew his nose loudly like a trumpet.

"It is bad enough that your mothers and fathers go to church, but you *young* fanatics have no right to hold religious meetings on Soviet soil," the police chief said indignantly.

For a moment the police chief remembered his mother. For years she had walked every Sunday to the Russian Orthodox Church. Then he shoved his memories aside. He had broken away from his mother's "foolish" religion long ago and had never been sorry. A *relighioznik* could never have become a police chief.

"Is is against the law then for us to meet to worship God?" Andrei asked respectfully.

"Well—of course our constitution says there is religious freedom for all Soviet citizens," the police chief sputtered, "but not for citizens under 18!" He pushed his handkerchief firmly back in his pocket.

The police chief was determined not to be sidetracked by Andrei's questions. "This disgraceful meeting cannot continue. We have come to send you home," he announced.

"But it is already so late at night. Can't we at least stay here till morning?" Andrei pleaded.

"No! Tonight!" the police chief shouted. "Perhaps a march down the cold, dark mountain will teach you *verruyuschiye* to think twice before you organize youth meetings. Such citizens! You are not fit to eat Soviet bread," he grumbled.

At that moment the other policeman stepped up and muttered something in the chief's ear.

"Search? Ah, yes, of course we should search them," the chief agreed.

Alexi heard the dreaded word "search" and his courage sank. *The Bibles—the Bibles!* he thought. *What will they do when they find the Bibles?* Frightened, Alexi wished he could seize his Bibles and flee down the mountain.

But suddenly the policeman who had done all the talking turned to Alexi. "You, boy. Let's see your pack!"

The police chief dumped Alexi's pack on the ground. He picked a black book from the pile and then a second black book. *"Bibliyi!"* He seemed stunned. "Search every pack in camp!" the police chief shouted.

Alexi wept silently. He thought of his father who had worked long into the night to bind Bibles for the Christians of Komsk. He thought of the other Christians in Narkutsk who had risked their freedom to print the Bibles on the secret press. And he thought of the boy from Komsk who had asked so eagerly, "Did you bring Bibles for us?"

An hour later, the two policemen had stacked all the Bibles in a huge heap in the center of the camp.

"Now you *will* stay on the mountain," the infuriated police chief raged at the young people. "You won't move a step until I find out where you got these Bibles. These Bibles weren't printed by our government," he added angrily.

The police chief shook his fist at Alexi who stood nearby. "By morning we will know where you young hooligans found your Bibles—or else!"

8.

Out of the Fiery Furnace

"Don't tell them anything," an older boy from Narkutsk managed to whisper to Alexi and Yuri. The furious police chief had meant what he said. One by one he questioned the teenagers around the campfire.

While he questioned one, the others softly sang hymns until the assistant policeman snapped, *"Dovolno*—enough of your foolish songs!"

"Who made you bring these Bibles?"

"Nobody. We knew the police took Bibles from the Christians in Komsk. We wanted to share ours."

"Who is your leader? Who tells you to do these fanatical things?"

"God is our Leader. We are followers of Jesus."

The sun went down late but arose again at three that morning. By sunrise, the police chief still had not finished the interrogations. He turned to his assistant who had been standing guard. "You hike down the mountain and bring some *druzhiniky*—civilian police back to help us," he ordered. "We can't march these hooligans home by ourselves. They might try to run away!"

By the time the sun was high above the mountain that morning, Alexi had heard everything but had said nothing. He knew that none of the young people had told the police chief anything about the Bibles or the secret press or the adults who printed the Russian Scriptures.

By late morning the policeman who had been sent away at daybreak to bring the *druzhiniky* back to guard the young people, returned. The *druzhiniky* straggled behind the assistant policeman in bewilderment.

Earlier that morning, most of them had been peacefully preparing to watch the worker's parade. Then they were suddenly summoned by the police and given red armbands to show they were *druzhiniky*—citizens on official duty.

The chief policeman stood on a stump and shouted at the young people. "You'll march down the trail two by two." He turned to the *druzhiniky*. "It is your duty to guard these hooligans well. It will be your fault if any of them flee into the forest!"

Obediently the young people stepped into line. And then they started to sing a verse of the song Alexi had taught the group the night before:

> Praise to God the Father and Son.
> Oh, how strong is His love for me.
> In love I serve Him.
> In His truth I find light.

"Stop that noise!" The chief yelled as he struggled to climb back up on the stump. But his voice was hoarse from so much shouting the night before, so he could not be heard above the 42 young people singing with all their might as they lined up for the march down the trail. The tired police chief shrugged his shoulders in resignation and the song continued.

The band of young people had already begun the long march down the mountain when one of the *druzhiniky,* whom the police chief had ordered to patrol up and down the line, passed by Yuri. He wore a blue sportsman's uniform.

"Alexi!" Yuri grabbed his friend's arm. "Look! That *druzhinik*—it is Pavel Akimovich—our coach!"

At that same moment Pavel Akimovich suddenly turned back and walked with determination toward the two boys and began marching beside them. "So it is Alexi Makarovitch and Yuri Samkov," he said, his voice almost muffled by the joyful singing of the other young people as they marched down the trail.

To Alexi's amazement, there was no reproach in his coach's voice. In fact, after several steps of silence, Pavel Akimovich turned to the boys. "This should not happen in a free country," he said sadly. "I am sorry." Then, as if he were afraid he had spoken too freely, the coach hurried on ahead.

But each time Pavel Akimovich patrolled the part of the line where Alexi and Yuri marched, he slowed to walk beside them. He listened closely to the joyous singing that had not stopped since the young Christians left the mountaintop.

"Do you really love your God so much?" he asked once, turning uncertainly to Alexi. "Sometimes I think

77

if there is such a God as you sing about—I would like to know him."

Before Alexi could answer, the police chief strode by. "You seem very friendly with your prisoners, Pavel Akimovich," he sneered.

"They are two students from my school," the coach said simply, but he spoke no more unguarded words and swiftly stepped ahead of the boys.

Alexi sang with the others the rest of the way, but he could not avoid the worry of what would happen when they finally reached the city. Would the police chief interrogate them again as he had threatened? Would he arrest them all?

As he marched, a new concern crowded into Alexi's thoughts. Pavel Akimovich had said he wished he "could know God." *Does he really mean that?* Alexi wondered.

By the time they neared the bottom of the trail, Alexi had made a decision. Somehow he must speak one more time with the coach.

"Pavel Akimovich!" Alexi managed to whisper as the coach marched by, the ugly red *druzhiniky* armband still tied firmly around his left arm. "Please!" Alexi knew he must speak quickly. "If you want to find God, listen to your shortwave radio—25 meter band—nine at night." That was all Alexi could whisper before another *druzhinik* pushed Pavel Akimovich roughly aside and reprimanded him for lingering too long in one place.

Alexi could never remember feeling so utterly exhausted as he did by the time they reached the bottom of the trail. Even Yuri, who never seemed to be tired, listlessly dragged his feet. "Do you think they will take us to the jail?" Yuri whispered, his voice worried.

The police chief surveyed the bedraggled band of young people, counting them carefully. "At least none of you was able to escape," he grumbled, ignoring the fact that none of them had tried.

"And now what should I do with you?" The police chief's voice was gruff but also weary. He leaned for support against a spruce tree.

At that moment, to Alexi's astonishment, Pavel Akimovich walked decisively to the police chief's side. "I have a suggestion," the coach spoke boldly. "You are tired," he said sympathetically to the police chief. "The young people are tired. If you march them to the police station, the whole town will know about this unfortunate incident. Why should we make such a fuss over these foolish Bibles? I am sure the young ones," Pavel Akimovich continued, glancing crossly at the weary group before him, "have learned their lesson. They will not soon forget this experience. You already have handled the situation brilliantly," he concluded, flattering the police chief.

Alexi was puzzled by the coach's cruel words. Pavel Akimovich had always been kinder than any of the other teachers at school—even when he knew Alexi and Yuri were Christians. But suddenly Alexi realized that the coach's words were cruel for a purpose—his intention was still kind.

The weary police chief considered the coach's suggestion. "But I still have not found out where they got the Bibles," he complained. He shifted back and forth on his aching legs and seemed to reconsider. "On the other hand, it *was* rather a firm punishment that I devised for these hooligans—interrogating them all night and then making them march down the mountain with no sleep!"

But the police chief himself also had not slept, and after 24 tiring hours he could not conceal his exhaustion. He wanted desperately to go home, but he could not let anyone suppose that he had failed.

He stood where the trail sloped up the hill, as if he hoped the additional height would give him more authority. "I have decided," he announced hoarsely, "to conclude your punishment—for now. I order you to return home immediately!" The chief shook his handkerchief threateningly at the young people as if to shoo them away. The young people quickly scattered.

"Alexi!" Mrs. Makarovitch clutched her son in her arms when he staggered in the apartment door and crumpled on the couch. "What has happened?" Alarm swept across her face.

Tanya flung her arms around her brother. "You—you look so frightened!" she exclaimed.

"We lost the Bibles—the police took them all!" Alexi said. He shuddered as he relived the cruel march.

"But praises to God they did not harm you." Mrs. Makarovitch embraced her son again.

Alexi thought he was too exhausted to talk, but when Poppa came home from the collective farm Alexi slowly told his family about the meeting on the mountains.

As he spoke, Momma repeatedly shook her head sadly. The scarf she wore slipped back on her head. Many times she reached across the table and stroked her son's hand. "Praise God, you are home, Alexi!"

"And we did not tell the police anything about the

Bibles. We prayed, and God helped us out of the fiery furnace," Alexi said, remembering the discussion at the youth meeting on Belovat Mountain.

"Thanks be to God, my son," Poppa said fervently. "Now we must pray for those who took the Bibles. We must have no bitterness in our hearts," he said firmly. "Instead, our hearts must be full of courage, praise, and love—even for our enemies."

Two days later, the Makarovitches were almost ready for bed when a knock thumped on the door.

"The police chief has come!" Alexi murmured, the terror of Belovat Mountain still strong in his memory.

Poppa unlatched the door. "Yuri, you've come so late!" Poppa exclaimed. The Makarovitches breathed easier. "Come in, come in."

"My father sent me, Mr. Makarovitch," Yuri explained. He sank onto the couch beside Alexi, breathless and shaken. "My father asked me to bring a message to you.

"When the general heard that the police took away the Bibles that we carried to the mountains . . ." Yuri paused, breathing hard. "Aleksandr Sergeyevich himself decided to take two suitcases of Bibles directly to the church in Komsk. He said the believers must have God's Word."

Alexi tensed when Yuri added, "Last night on the way to Komsk, the general was stopped by the police!"

81

9.

The Interrupted Journey

"Did the police search the general's suitcase?" Alexi finally forced himself to ask.

Yuri nodded silently. "And they know the Bibles were printed here in Narkutsk. They are holding Aleksandr Sergeyevich at the police station until the court trial," Yuri said, his choked voice nearly a whisper.

Tanya, who had been standing beside her mother while listening to Yuri's story about the general, started to sob. Mrs. Makarovitch tried to comfort her daughter, but tears trickled from her own eyes and she could only hug Tanya tightly.

Poppa paced the room. "Does your father know to which prison they will take the general, Yuri?" he asked soberly.

"No," Yuri replied. "As soon as father heard what had happened to the general, he hurried to the police station and asked if he could speak with citizen Aleksandr Sergeyevich. But the police know father is a believer. They shouted, 'You stay away from Aleksandr Sergeyevich until this trial is over.'"

Alexi pictured the general hunched again in a prison cell with no other Christians to comfort him. "It isn't fair, Poppa," Alexi declared indignantly. "Our Soviet constitution says that all citizens have a right to a just and open trial. Our school lessons teach that."

Alexi snatched up the textbook that lay on the table ready for tomorrow's lesson. "Listen! This is what it says: 'All citizens, irrespective of social status or office, are equal before the law. This equality is unaffected by nationality, Party membership or *religious beliefs.*'" Alexi emphasized the last two words.

"What our Soviet constitution says and what our government sometimes does to Christians are two different things," Mrs. Makarovitch said, more bitterly than Alexi had ever heard his mother speak.

"Sh! Sh! All of you." Poppa held out his arms as if he would enclose his family within their safe circle and comfort them if he could. He reached for the Bible which the general had given them. Slowly Poppa read, "Thou therefore endure hardness, as a good soldier of Jesus Christ . . . ."

Then, closing the black covers of the Bible, he said, "And now we will pray for Aleksandr Sergeyevich." The family and Yuri knelt on the brown painted wood floor. "Oh, Lord, *podkrepi yevo*—strengthen him," Momma whispered softly while her husband prayed aloud for their brother in Christ.

The next week the Christians from the house meeting in Narkutsk went bravely every day to the

84

police station. Every day they asked the same questions: "Is Aleksandr Sergeyevich still here at the police station? Please, can we just speak with him briefly? In which prison will he be held? When will his trial be? What are the charges against him?" But the officials gave no answers.

Some of the Christians took parcels of food to the police station. Some took warm clothes wrapped in a bundle. The babushka who had wanted to give Aleksandr Sergeyevich a bouquet of lilacs months before, trudged now to the police station—a bouquet of flowers in her arms for the general.

"Please, give them to Aleksandr Sergeyevich," she pleaded. But the police only turned the babushka roughly away from the station.

After a week of uncertainty, the police authorities finally admitted that the general was still being held inside the police station with other prisoners. "But no visitors are allowed inside," they insisted. The case was closed. The general's brothers and sisters in Christ could only pray.

For months Yuri and Alexi had planned for the last day of June when school would be finished. Summer in Siberia stretched invitingly ahead. "We'll hike in the mountains and fish in the river," Yuri had schemed enthusiastically. He had lived all his life in Siberia.

But now on the last day in June, when Alexi and Yuri said good-bye to Olga Yakovna, they could not concentrate on their summer adventures. "If only we could at least *see* the general," Yuri groaned.

On the first day of vacation, Alexi woke early and looked at his wristwatch. Four-thirty. The hot summer sun already stood in the sky, beckoning through the lacy curtains.

"Sleep, my little *dyetki*—sleep. This is your vacation," Momma had urged last night when she kissed Tanya and Alexi good-night. But Alexi could not sleep. Restlessly, he worried about the general. *Could the general see the bright sun inside the police station?* Alexi wondered.

Suddenly Alexi made a decision. Somehow he had to try to see the general just once more. If they took Aleksandr Sergeyevich away to prison, he might never see him again. He pulled his shoes from under the couch and swiftly put on his clothes. Stepping softly, careful not to awaken Tanya who was still sleeping soundly across the room, he slipped out the door of the apartment.

Only the night before Alexi had gone with his father and two of the men from the church to carry a food parcel to the police station. He thought he knew the way well. Swiftly he strode through the still sleepy streets.

Although it was only five a.m. by the time Alexi reached the subway entrance, a woman in a dark blue suit sat in a booth selling train tickets for three kopecks apiece.

Alexi clutched his ticket and bent to check the lighted map of the city. "Mirny Square," he mumbled aloud as he traced the route to the police station.

"It's down the escalator—the track on the left," the woman in blue said, motioning helpfully toward the long tunnel that led to the train.

By the time Alexi stepped off the train and stood in front of the gray, faceless building that was the police station, he felt his hopes, that had risen bright with the sun, beginning to sink.

The police station squatted dark and desolate inside Mirny Square. Questions raced through Alexi's mind. *Are there people inside? Where do they keep the general? Will they let me in?* Cautiously he approached the grim building.

But at that moment the front door of the station swung open and a man stepped out. Alexi stopped. Four more men walked solemnly side by side through the door in a kind of formation.

When Alexi saw the general he cried out, "Aleksandr Sergeyevich!" forgetting that he stood only a few yards from the police station.

The policeman nearest the general saw Alexi and shouted, "What are you doing up so early, boy? This is no place for spectators. Move along!"

The general glanced eagerly when he heard his name, but he did not wave. In an instant Alexi noticed that the general was handcuffed to the man walking beside him. The man who marched behind was also handcuffed to the man at his side.

The prisoners, handcuffed to their police guards, groped slowly down the steps, unable to see in the sudden glare of sunlight. Cautiously, Alexi edged closer. He tried to hide behind a car parked near the building. "This is a good time to transfer them, comrade," he overheard one policeman say to the other. "Those Christians aren't going to be pestering us this early in the morning."

Alexi waited until the police and their prisoners had turned a corner. Then he followed at a distance. Every time the Makarovitches attended the Christian house meetings they walked cautiously. But with a stab of understanding that made him feel far older than his 13 years, Alexi knew that today was different.

Slowly the streets began filling with workers. Alexi followed closer to the prisoners and their guards—careful not to lose sight of the general. An old man with an armful of *Pravda* newspapers also pushed near the prisoners. He put down his bundle of papers and paused to stare at the strange procession. "Out of the way, old man!" one of the police guards said, shoving him aside.

"I wish Yuri was here—I wish I had asked Tanya to come," Alexi thought. "What will Poppa think? Momma will be worried."

A few blocks farther, the police halted their prisoners at a bus stop. Were the police going to take their prisoners on a bus? Alexi poked his head through the long line of waiting people. One man swung a string bag full of fish in Alexi's direction. "Stay in line, comrade!" he shouted irritably.

To Alexi's relief, the police marched their prisoners past the bus stop. Suddenly they turned up the street that led to the railroad station. Alexi followed frantically. *Where will they take the general now?* he worried.

He thought of the terrible remote prison outside Narkutsk that he had once heard an old man tell about who had been imprisoned there ten years earlier. The old man's fingers had shriveled from frostbite, and he trembled at the memory of his years in exile. *"Strashna, strashna*—it is a terrible place," Alexi had heard him say.

But the police did not stop at the railroad station.

They marched another two blocks to the edge of the city, and then halted their prisoners in front of a walled building that Alexi had always thought was a factory.

One of the policemen pulled a heavy chain of keys from his pocket and bent to unlock the heavy metal gate. As the guards started to push their prisoners inside the gate, Alexi ran toward the general.

"Aleksandr Sergeyevich! Aleksandr Sergeyevich!" Alexi tried to throw his arms around the general. "Please! Don't go inside!"

"Alexi! Little brother, Alexi!" The general tried to put his arms around Alexi, but the ugly steel handcuffs held him back. Concern clouded the joy in the general's eyes. He spoke quickly. "I am so glad to see you, little brother, but you must go. It is dangerous . . ."

A furious policeman pulled Alexi away. "This is not a place for children!" he shouted. "Go away! Out of here! Immediately!" He shoved Alexi away and clanked the gate in his face.

10.

A Message from the General

Bewildered, Alexi clung to the gate. He peered through the metal bars but they were welded tightly together and he could see little. Disappointment swept over him as he stumbled from the gate. How could he leave now? He had been so certain he would at least be able to talk with the general.

Alexi surveyed the building from where he stood. The gate was high and a black iron fence seemed to enclose the whole building. Twice Alexi followed the fence around until finally he found one place where the metal bars were spaced slightly wider apart.

Squeezing his face close to the bars to peer between them, he could see a concrete courtyard circling the building inside. A few forlorn trees rose between cracks of the concrete. Men in gray prisoner uniforms strolled for exercise in the courtyard. Some leaned against the metal fence.

Alexi searched the men's faces for the general, but Aleksandr Sergeyevich was not yet there. Disappointed, Alexi turned from the fence. He stopped to think beside a tall poplar tree across the street. *I should go home,* he thought. *My family will be frightened.* He felt hungry and scared himself. But at that moment, Alexi glanced up and noticed that the tree grew high above the prison wall.

Quickly Alexi climbed the tree. Through the drooping branches he could see clearly down into the courtyard. "I'll stay here and wait until the general comes," he resolved. But by noon, he still had not seen the general in the courtyard. And Alexi, who had eaten nothing that morning, soon felt weak and hungry. He wished he had put a *bulochka* in his pocket.

Despite his hunger, Alexi stayed—staring, scanning the courtyard for some sign of the general. Smoke rose from the chimney of the big building. Every hour a new group of men came out in the courtyard, and the others were summoned back inside.

By late afternoon, Alexi grew so drowsy he thought he might tumble from the tree. Just when he was sure he could watch no longer and was almost ready to climb down the tree, the general walked from the door of the big building into the courtyard.

Alexi scurried down from the tree. He pressed his face against the fence. "Please, Lord, help Aleksandr Sergeyevich to walk this way," he prayed. The general, who paced the courtyard absorbed in his own thoughts, strolled several feet from the fence.

"Brother Aleksandr!" Alexi whispered urgently through the fence. Startled, the general turned. His anxiety brightened to a smile when he saw Alexi.

Alexi pressed his face close to the fence. He tried to push his hand through the metal bars to touch the general, but the space was too small.

"Dear Alexi," the general spoke softly through the fence. "What boy in all of Narkutsk would care so much to stay by me as you have! But now you must go home, Alexi. This is a city work prison. The authorities will be angry if they discover you here."

"A work prison?" Alexi asked.

"A prison, yes, but there is a factory inside," the general explained. "The authorities tell me I will work here until it is time for my trial."

"Trial!" The ugly word filled Alexi with fear. He gazed at the general through the bars. "What will they do to you, Aleksandr Sergeyevich?" He struggled to hold back tears.

"Your face is so sad, little brother," the general said sympathetically. "Is it for me you are sad?" he asked.

Alexi nodded.

"But, Alexi, for a Christian soldier all things happen for a purpose." The general glanced at the guard who dozed in the hot afternoon sun across the courtyard. Then he spoke more slowly: "You see, Alexi, I too was at first filled with sorrow when the police arrested me and took me to the police station. I have been in prison before. I feel too old—too tired to travel this hard way again.

"The first two days I was in prison," the general sighed, "I prayed constantly to God. I begged God to break open the door of my cell and send an angel to set me free—as God did for the apostle Peter 2,000 years ago.

"But then, little brother," the general smiled, "I

listened. God spoke to me, and now I am at peace. Jesus will walk with me every step—even if I must carry a cross.

"I see doubt still in your eyes, Alexi," the general spoke kindly through the fence. "I will tell you a story and then you will understand.

"When I was in prison three years ago, the authorities sent me many miles from here to a prison camp deep in the forest. There were 200 prisoners. All day we worked hard in the forest—cutting trees and mining coal. Even in freezing weather we worked. By night, we were exhausted. Most of the prisoners fell in bed as soon as they could.

"One of the prisoners, who had been a professor before he was arrested, watched me pray every night. 'Do you really believe there is a God?' the professor asked one day. 'Do you truly believe he hears you when you pray?'

"I told the professor about God. I had no Bible, but I was glad I had hidden the words of the Bible here, little brother," the general said, holding his hand over his heart.

"Soon the other prisoners began asking questions. I told them about Jesus. I made a *balalaika*—a Russian guitar—from scraps of wood and I sang songs about God. Every night I told the prisoners stories from the Bible.

" 'I have tried everything in life, but nothing has given me peace in my heart,' the professor told me through tears one night after I told the prisoners the story of the prodigal son. 'Could I become a *verruyuschiy*—here in prison?'

"'A man who was a thief said, 'God sent you here to

tell us about Jesus. If you had not come, I would never have heard about God's Son.'

"First the professor became a Christian. Then the thief believed. Then three other prisoners wanted to follow Christ," the general said. "By winter seven prisoners had believed in Jesus.

" 'Now we must be baptized,' the believers insisted. 'We must not wait.' So there in the prison camp," the general continued, a faraway, happy look in his eyes, "I baptized seven new believers. We chopped a hole in the ice on the lake for our baptismal service.

"After the baptismal service, the new Christians wanted to celebrate communion. We saved pieces of bread from our small prisoner portions. One winter day, inside a dark tunnel of the coal mine, the seven of us knelt and shared communion—we remembered the broken body of Christ.

"I will never forget those days." He seemed lost in his memories. "No, Alexi." He straightened from his stooped position speaking through the fence. "You must not pity me. The last time I was put in prison, God arranged it for a purpose. If I am sentenced again to prison, after the trial, then again it will be for God's purpose," the general said.

The guard who napped in a corner of the courtyard stirred. "I must go, Alexi," the general whispered. "Tell the other brothers and sisters that you have seen me. Tell them that Jesus is with me. Good-bye. Go with God, little brother." The general turned from the fence.

But then he suddenly came back and bent again to whisper to Alexi: "One more thing—do not forget to tell them, Alexi. Tell them they must take bread to the believers in Komsk! The believers must have Bibles!"

11.

The Coach's Defense

Alexi stumbled away from the city work prison in a daze. He wound his way toward the subway station. Instead of feeling reassured by the general's encouraging story, he felt frustrated—and angry.

"The general is a good man," Alexi fumed. "He fought for our country. Poppa said he is a Soviet hero. But because he is a Christian, he is treated like a criminal." Bitterly Alexi booted a stone that had rolled on the sidewalk.

As if he himself were trapped in a deep, dark prison, he struggled with his thoughts. "Why did the general admit to the police that he was a believer? He could be a secret Christian." Alexi felt doubts closing like a dungeon around him as he returned to the family's apartment.

"Alexi! Where have you been?" Tanya threw her

arms around her brother. "Momma was crying when she left for work this morning because you were not home! Poppa was worried too. You have been gone so many hours!" Tanya's cheeks were streaked with tears as she opened wide the apartment door.

"I'm sorry, Tanya," Alexi mumbled, the dark mood of despair still locked around him. "I'll walk up the street and meet Momma and Poppa when they come from work. I'll tell them I'm home."

"But where were you? What were you doing? Why didn't you wake me so I could go too?" Tanya trailed along, eager to hear about her brother's adventures.

Later that night when Poppa and Alexi sat alone in the kitchen sipping tea, Alexi complained, "It is just not fair, Poppa. The general is such a good man. Why doesn't God help him?" Alexi spoke almost angrily.

"There are many things we Christians in Russia don't understand, Alexi," Poppa admitted, squeezing a thin slice of lemon into his glass of hot tea. "In my lifetime I have not always understood God's ways. But this does not prevent me from believing that God understands.

"When I was your age, for example," Poppa said, slowly sipping the weak tea, "I wanted to be an engineer more than anything else. Later, when I graduated from secondary school and after I had served in the army, I enrolled in the university. During my second year at the university I became a believer. In my last year at the university the authorities discovered I was a *verruyuschiy*. 'You must choose—either God or your diploma,' they told me."

Poppa paused reflectively. "I chose God, Alexi. Although I had only a few months to finish before graduation, I never received my diploma—but I have told you that part of the story before.

"There is something that I have *not* told you before." Mr. Makarovitch spoke earnestly, leaning toward his son. He glanced into the other room. Tanya and Momma still had not returned from their walk in the park. "After the authorities expelled me from the university, they sent me to a prison in northern Siberia."

"Poppa—*you* were in prison! In Siberia?" Alexi asked in astonishment.

"Yes, Alexi, I, too, was in prison." Poppa's hand trembled on the tea glass. "Those days under Stalin were even more difficult than now. And northern Siberia is not like Narkutsk. The Arctic is a frozen, forsaken place." Poppa shuddered. "I was put in prison only because I was a believer and a good student. They said a Christian student was a disgrace to a Soviet university."

The same helpless fury Alexi had felt at the fence of the city work prison surged through him. The image of the black prison bars rose up again before him. "It isn't *fair!*" Alexi clenched his fists.

"You are a young soldier of the Cross, Alexi," Poppa said thoughtfully. "There are still many battles ahead that you do not yet understand. But a good soldier does not stop when the battle hurts. He only obeys orders more carefully than ever.

"You see, Alexi," Poppa explained, "most people in Russia are living for one kingdom—the kingdom of earth. We Christians also strive to be good citizens of that kingdom—our own dear Russia.

"But first we are citizens of God's Kingdom."

Poppa's eyes shone as if he could see that holy country.

"That day in the university, I chose to be a good soldier of God's Kingdom," Poppa said softly. "I have not been sorry. After prison God gave me a job as an engineer, even though I had never graduated."

Poppa paused, "And now I work at the collective farm." He shrugged. "I am not sorry. I have been able to tell many of the workers about Jesus."

That night in bed Alexi felt the prison of his own fear and frustration. But slowly, as he prayed, the black oppression lifted and light streamed through his troubled thoughts like the sun in a dungeon.

"I want to follow You, Jesus," he whispered. "I want to walk in Your way—like Poppa—like the general."

The general! With a jolt, Alexi remembered the general's message to his father: "Do not forget to take Bibles to the believers in Komsk!"

"But who will take the Bibles?" Alexi worried.

The next morning when Alexi told his father about the general's message, Poppa was perplexed. "It would be hopeless now for any of the men from the house meeting to go." Poppa considered the problem. "Since the police stopped the general, they have been searching more suspiciously than ever to stop the Bibles from being printed. But still, somehow we must deliver the Bibles to the Christians in Komsk."

While his father spoke, Alexi struggled with a daring plan. The general had tried to deliver the Bibles to Komsk. Aleksandr Sergeyevich was willing to risk everything so the Christians could have God's Words. "It is God's will." The general's words returned to Alexi.

"I know how we could deliver the Bibles to Komsk, Poppa," Alexi spoke with determination. "Yuri and I could carry them. We could go together on the train . . . ."

It was another week before the trial of Aleksandr Sergeyevich was held. When the trial was held, the police tried to keep the time and place a secret. They invited citizens to attend, whom they were certain were not Christians, to fill up the empty seats of the courtroom.

On the first day of the trial, the judge, a frowning man who wore glasses, waited for the accused at the front of the small courtroom under a gold and red emblem of a hammer and sickle.

When Aleksandr Sergeyevich, pale and weary, but with the same strong light in his eyes, appeared before the judge, a hush fell on the crowd. "But he is such a kindly looking man. You can see he's no vodka-drinking hoodlum!" a babushka who had been brought by the police to fill up a seat in the courtroom whispered loudly.

"Tikho! Silence in this courtroom!" the judge shouted. "Now, procurator," the judge addressed the lawyer, "you may proceed with your case against the accused, Aleksandr Sergeyevich."

The procurator was a woman. Stout and unsmiling, she rose to face the general. She held a sheaf of papers in her hand. "Aleksandr Sergeyevich," she addressed the general sternly, "you are charged with the distribution of literature containing deliberately false statements slandering the Soviet state.

"Since you insist you will stand for your own defense

rather than accept the services of our defense procurator, you may now proceed." The woman could not suppress a sarcastic smile.

Aleksandr Sergeyevich rose to face the lawyer. His deep, gentle voice filled the courtroom. "I am a loyal Soviet citizen. I am innocent of distributing anti-Soviet literature. The Bibles I carried do not contain anti-Soviet statements. I know that I stand before this court today only because I am a Christian!"

"Because you are a Christian!" the woman procurator shrieked, forgetting court decorum. "In our country there is freedom of religion." She glanced at the judge, who nodded approvingly. "How dare you slander our Soviet government!"

Aleksandr Sergeyevich stood silently for several seconds as if he were seriously considering the procurator's words. "Citizen procurator," he said, leaning forward earnestly, "if I deny God—if I promise not to be a Christian—then is there a possibility I could go free?"

"Why, I am sure something could be arranged," the procurator replied, ignoring the startled spectators in the courtroom behind her. "If you would be willing to sign a statement that you no longer believe in God and that you will stop printing Bibles . . ."

"So you see, comrades," Aleksandr Sergeyevich's voice thundered beyond the procurator to the bewildered crowd in the courtroom, "it *is* my faith for which I am being tried before this court. It is *only* because I am a believer." The general leaned toward the silent crowd which listened raptly. "But I would not trade that belief for all the roubles in the world."

With those words the courtroom filled with

commotion. "Even if he is a Christian, he is still a Soviet citizen! He has broken no law! He deserves a fair trial!"

His fist like a hammer, the judge banged furiously on the desk before him. "Silence, citizens!" he shouted. "If anyone wishes to offer evidence in this courtroom, he must speak in an orderly fashion! Of course, I am sure no one would want to oppose the opinion of this court." The judge settled himself smugly against the bench.

But at that moment, to everyone's amazement, a citizen sitting on the back bench of the courtroom stood up. Uneasily the judge and procurator followed the man's steps as he marched firmly to the front of the room and halted before the judge.

"Citizen judge," he said, standing straight and sure, "I request premission to speak in defense of citizen Aleksandr Sergeyevich."

"Well, I did not really expect that anyone would want to speak in defense of the accused," the judge fumbled. But then he saw the expectant faces of the crowd before him. "Well, since I did open the court to witnesses . . ." He hesitated.

"Thank you, citizen judge." The man straightened and turned to face the courtroom. "For many years I have known Aleksandr Sergeyevich," the man said. "I served under Aleksandr Sergeyevich in the Red Army. I was proud to serve under a general who personally knew Lenin."

"Lenin!" A gasp rose from the courtroom. "The accused knew Lenin! The accused is a general!"

The woman procurator's face was blotchy and red and she looked as if she might explode, but the witness continued speaking before the procurator could interrupt.

"As a young soldier, I served under General Aleksandr Sergeyevich. He served our country well in the war against the enemy. He loves Mother Russia . . ." The witness paused as the courtroom broke into confusion.

12.

Mission Accomplished

"Poppa, Yuri and I—we could take the Bibles to the Christians in Komsk. I think it is God's will." Even Tanya was surprised at the certainty in her brother's voice.

"Perhaps it *is* God's will, Alexi," Poppa said slowly. "Perhaps God wants you and Yuri to finish the mission the general began."

"But Ivan . . ." Momma had bravely tried to say nothing, but she could not stay silent. "Alexi is only a boy. And we know what happened to the general." Her gray shawl drooped from her shoulders. "What will they do if they discover the Bibles?"

Poppa placed his strong, rough hand on top of his wife's smaller one. "The authorities are watching constantly, Galya. If one of us adults tries to take Bibles to Komsk, we will probably not get past the train station."

Poppa tried to conceal his own worry and comfort his wife. "The mission will be a secret. The authorities will not know. We will pray and trust that the police will *not* discover the Bibles Alexi and Yuri carry to Komsk."

"And I'm 13 now, Momma," Alexi said, trying to encourage his mother.

"Of course I want to go!" Yuri declared when Alexi told his friend about the plan to deliver Bibles to Komsk. "But first I must ask my father."

Eight days later, when the newly printed Bibles were safely stowed in their suitcases, Mr. Makarovitch and the two boys walked together toward the railroad station. "Poppa, when you visit the work prison, will you tell Aleksandr Sergeyevich that we have taken the Bibles to the believers in Komsk?" Alexi asked.

"I will try, Alexi—if the general has not already been taken away to the trial. If only the police would tell us when the trial will be and where it will be held," Poppa repeated the troubling question for which the Christians had not been able to find the answers.

"Where are you boys going with those big suitcases?" a porter asked when Yuri and Alexi reached the train station. He grabbed Alexi's suitcase and shoved it up the high steps of the train.

"We're going to Komsk, comrade," Alexi replied politely, but his heart thumped as he watched the porter hoist his suitcase up the steps. Would the porter wonder why the suitcase was so heavy?

"Let's look for an empty compartment," Yuri whispered as the boys shouldered their way down the narrow, smoky corridor of the train. But the compartments were filling fast. The train only stopped once a day in Narkutsk.

In the last car, the boys found a compartment with two empty seats. The other four seats were occupied by a smiling family traveling to Lake Okal for a holiday.

"Here, let me help you boys with those heavy suitcases," the father of the family said, standing when he saw the boys struggling to lift their suitcases to the wire rack overhead.

Alexi hesitated. He was afraid for anyone to touch the suitcases with the Bibles. But the man was only trying to be helpful, he reminded himself. He remembered Poppa's last words when they said good-bye several blocks before the train station. "Be a good soldier, Alexi. Trust in Jesus. Don't be afraid."

The two small children who belonged to the family going to Lake Okal watched the big boys sitting in the seats across from them with curious eyes as the train rumbled from the station. But their parents leaned back against the hard seats and soon fell asleep.

Alexi and Yuri said little as the train struggled along the moutain slope toward Komsk. Somehow it seemed safer not to speak. But when the train slowed at a wooden shack beside the railroad track with a sign *TAMOZHNIK* on the front, Alexi poked Yuri. *"Tamozhnik*—inspectors!" He pointed apprehensively toward the sign.

Two men in baggy blue uniforms sauntered out of the shack and climbed onto the train. Through the window, Alexi could see the very same word, *TAMOZHNIK* written across their caps.

"What if the inspectors check the suitcases?" Yuri whispered worriedly.

Alexi leaned stiffly back against the straight seat.

Alexi, who sat by the compartment door, saw the two inspectors first. They were moving slowly down the hall, stopping at each compartment on the way. One of the men held a large blue notebook in his hand.

The two children in the seats across from Yuri and Alexi peeked out the door of the compartment. "Momma! Poppa! The inspectors are coming!" they squealed.

"Will the inspector take my *kukla* away?" the little girl started to cry and crawled into her mother's lap, clutching her doll tighter.

"Of course they won't," the mother comforted the child.

By the time the inspectors reached the compartment next door, Alexi heard the men's voices clearly. "Everybody open your suitcase," one of the inspectors commanded.

"But we aren't crossing a border, comrade. Why must we be searched?" someone objected.

"Just do as you are told!" the inspector snapped. "Our orders are to search everything today."

"Everything!" Alexi heard the inspector's words roar like a train over him. Terrified, he remembered what had happened when the general's Bibles were discovered. "Pray, Yuri. Pray!" Alexi's voice shook.

The suitcases in the compartment next door were clanked shut. The inspectors' dreaded footsteps thudded nearer the boys' compartment.

"Do you all belong to the same family?" the inspector asked as he shoved into the compartment. The little girl started to cry again. "Come, come—we haven't all day," the inspector muttered impatiently.

"Open your suitcases. We will search everything."

Obediently Alexi stood to pull his suitcase to the floor. The inspector reached for the handle. But suddenly a shrill, squealing sound tore through the train. The train screeched along the steel tracks. Then the train snapped to a stop, and in a second Alexi was slammed into the seat across the aisle.

"Momma, the boys are falling on top of me!" the little girl shrieked. Passengers in other compartments who had been hurled to the floor started to scream, "What happened? Are they trying to kill us?"

The inspector, who had been knocked to the floor by the sudden stop, stood to his feet. "What's wrong with this stupid train now?" he shouted, brushing dust from his blue uniform.

Finally, a shaken voice sounded over the loudspeaker: "Attention, comrades. Forgive us, but we have a little problem. The brakes have locked on the train. All railroad workers will disembark immediately and assist with the repair of the train. All passengers will remain in their compartments," the voice ordered over the loudspeaker.

"We're inspectors—not laborers. Who do they think they are ordering us around?" one inspector grumbled loudly to the other.

"These stupid trains are always breaking down," the first inspector said, stooping to pick up his notebook that had tumbled to the floor. Reluctantly both men trudged out of the compartment.

With quiet praise to God, the boys quickly pushed their suitcases back to the secure rack. But suddenly a new fear shook Alexi. "What if the inspectors return and finish the search?" he whispered to Yuri.

After much pounding, complaining, and prodding with crowbars, the brakes were unlocked. Workmen, grimy and grumbling, climbed back onto the train. Through the windows, Alexi saw the two inspectors—their uniforms were smudged and their faces were streaked with sweat. They stepped onto the train just as it started with a jolt.

"Only 40 minutes to Komsk." Alexi checked his watch as the inspectors disappeared down the hall in the opposite direction. "Only 30 minutes now . . . 20 minutes . . ."

When the train was just ten minutes from Komsk, the inspectors plodded up the narrow corridor toward the boys' compartment. "We're so close to Komsk—they won't search us now," Alexi hoped desperately.

But in seconds, the disgruntled inspectors were inside their compartment. One inspector pointed to Alexi's suitcase. "Unlock it," he said, but he glanced indifferently at the two boys as if they were probably too young to carry anything significant in their suitcases. He stared at the impressive suitcases of the family across the aisle.

Alexi tried to stop his fingers from trembling as he unlatched the suitcase. Slowly he lifted the lid. Inside lay the Bibles. Only that morning Poppa had carefully wrapped them in newspaper and placed them in the suitcase.

The inspector looked inside. "So you like to read *Pravda* do you, boy? It's a good thing somebody reads the newspapers in this country!" the inspector muttered, still fuming from the disgrace of being forced to help fix the train wheels.

The inspectors turned to the family across the aisle and thoroughly checked their luggage. The inspectors were still complaining to each other when they left the compartment.

Alexi slumped back against the hard seat. He trembled when he thought of what could have happened. "Thank You, Lord," he said silently. The suitcases were safe.

Finally the decrepit train heaved into the station. "KOMSK," a huge black and white sign with the name of the city, was posted on the platform.

Inside the train station, the boys bought *peroghi* for a few kopecks. They ate the hot buns filled with spicy meat, felt their strength return, and waited for darkness. By the time the boys stepped out on the street with their suitcases, it was nine o'clock at night. The Siberian sun still had not fallen completely behind the mountains.

Alexi fumbled in his pocket for the address of the church—920 Gorky Street. "We will take a streetcar as close to the house where the believers meet as we can. Then we'll walk the rest of the way through the darkness to the house," he repeated his father's instructions.

At 920 Gorky Street, the boys cautiously pushed open the gate into the church courtyard. From inside the house, singing like ocean waves rose to meet them. "The meeting has already begun," Yuri whispered.

Alexi tiptoed to the house door and silently shoved it open. Quietly the boys explored the entry hall where they waited. The Christians, who had walked to the meeting in the cool summer night, had hung their coats on hooks that covered each side of the hall. The meeting room was several feet beyond the coat closet.

Alexi had an idea. He held up a Bible—just the size to slip easily into a pocket. "Let's put the Bibles in the coats," he suggested. "They won't hear us, and we can leave before they finish praying. If there are any informers from the government at the meeting, they won't know who brought the Bibles. If anybody asks the Christians where the Bibles came from, they won't know either."

"It's a good plan," Yuri said, silently unlatching his suitcase. Swiftly he placed a Bible in a pocket of each coat along the rack. "We have to *hurry*—before they finish praying," Yuri whispered as he worked.

But the prayers of the Christians were long. "Help our brother, Aleksandr Sergeyevich," they prayed. "May he speak Your words when he comes to the trial . . ."

When the boys had emptied the last Bibles from their suitcases, they stole softly out the door of the house church. "I wish we could have met the Christians," Yuri said when they were safely outside.

"I wish we could see their faces when they find the Bibles," Alexi added, smiling at the surprise waiting for the believers.

The boys were just ready to step out of the courtyard into the street—their mission safely accomplished— when suddenly the courtyard gate swung toward them.

"The police!" Alexi thought and trembled. Or was it the police? An awesome man with smiling eyes stood before the boys.

"Aleksandr Sergeyevich!" both boys exclaimed together, flinging themselves on the general.

"I see you have safely brought Bread to the believers, little brothers. You have completed your mission." The general embraced the boys.

"But Aleksandr Sergeyevich, how—when—? We thought you were still in prison—or at the trial," Yuri exclaimed, his voice choked by surprise and emotion.

Quietly Aleksandr Sergeyevich led the boys to a corner of the courtyard. "We must not disturb the meeting." He walked softly in his heavy boots.

"It is a miracle, my young brothers," the general said. "The procurator and judge were ready to sentence me to prison when suddenly," the general's eyes sparkled, "a soldier who served under my command when I was a general in the Soviet army spoke in my defense. He told the judge I was innocent—that I had broken no Soviet laws.

"The judge and procurator were angry at the man who used to be a soldier," the general continued. "But the people in the courtroom believed his witness. They started to shout at the judge and the procurator, 'This man is innocent! He should be set free!' "

"Who was the man who testified for you?" Yuri asked.

"The man who used to be my soldier is your hockey coach." The general smiled.

"Pavel Akimovich!" the boys gasped together.

"Pavel Akimovich has become a Christian," the general said. "That was why he walked to the front of the courtroom to defend me."

"Pavel Akimovich—my coach—a Christian?" Alexi was astonished.

"It should not be such a surprise to you, Alexi," the general said. "You told Pavel Akimovich about the

116

Christian radio broadcasts that day you marched down from Belovat Mountain. Pavel Akimovich listened. Now he believes."

"Did the judge set you free forever, Aleksandr Sergeyevich?" To Alexi it seemed that everything must end well on this wonderful day.

"Not forever, little brothers," the general spoke sadly. "I've been released only temporarily. The judge has scheduled another trial in a different court. I must return to Narkutsk soon."

As the general spoke, the Christians started to sing inside the house church.

> When we finish the fierce battle here on earth,
> Soldiers of the cross of Christ,
> We will come to our holy, heavenly home . . . .

EPILOGUE

Alexi's Secret Mission is the story of one Christian family living in the Soviet Union—a society that is officially atheistic.

Although this book is fiction, the incidents on which the story is based are factual.

The Makarovitch family, for example, is fictional, but their circumstances are a compilation of those endured by many Christian families whom we met in the Soviet Union.

My husband and I remember the couple with ten children whom we met in northern Russia. They live in four rooms but still find space to hold Christian meetings in their home.

In southern Russia, we met a man who was converted while attending the university. He was told, as was Mr. Makarovitch, "You must choose—it's either God or your diploma."

And everywhere in the Soviet Union, parents told us, "It is *ochen trudno*—very difficult for Christian children in our country."

The story of the general, Aleksandr Sergeyevich, is modeled after a Christian general who knew Lenin as a young man. He was converted while listening to Christian radio broadcasts when he was stationed in Siberia. Before his conversion, the general was an honored hero of Soviet society. After his conversion, he was stripped of his military title and treated as an outcast.

When we traveled in Russia, we met many people, like the general, who had been led to Christ through the Gospel broadcasts from missionary radio stations. We met many Christian families who told us, "We listen to your broadcasts on our knees. When you pray, we pray. When you sing, we sing. We copy down the words you read from the Scriptures."

Although there are few hymnbooks available in their country, Russian believers love to sing, and they are constantly writing new hymns. These hymns are often hand-copied, widely circulated, and sung by Christians all over the Soviet Union.

The hymn that the Makarovitches sang, for example, was written by a Christian in a Siberian prison. This hymn is cherished by Christians across Russia.

The dilemma of Russian Christians, like the Makarovitches and the believers in Komsk who wanted Bibles but could not buy any in bookstores in their own country, is very real. There are still many Christian families across Russia who do not own a Bible or any other Christian book.

In the past 45 years, the Soviet government has authorized only token printings of Bibles. At the most, 120,000 Bibles and 45,000 New Testaments have been printed. This amount is totally inadequate to supply Russia's estimated 40 million Russian Orthodox adherents, more than 6 million Protestants, and 3.5 million Roman Catholics.

Because Bibles are so desperately scarce and since the Soviet government refuses permission to print them in adequate quantities, some Christians, like the believers in this story, have begun printing Bibles secretly on hidden presses. Believers in Russia call their press the *khristianin*.

In our travels, we met Russian Christians who had helped print Bibles on this hidden press. We became well acquainted with one family who helped bind the Bibles after they were printed. The true experiences of these believers have provided much of the background for the story of *Alexi's Secret Mission*.

Once the Bibles are printed, the hazards of distributing them are just as risky as I have described in this story. In Russia, Christians told us of their constant attempts to obtain official permission to print and distribute the Bibles openly. Soviet authorities have answered this plea by punishing the Christians who help print and deliver Bibles.

Russian believers in several places told us about a 21-year-old girl who was arrested while she was delivering a suitcase filled with Bibles by train to believers in another town. Russian Christians asked us to tell believers outside the U.S.S.R. about this girl. "Ask the brothers and sisters in the West to pray for her," they said.

In this story, the Christians in Narkutsk meet in a house. The young people from Narkutsk and Komsk hold a youth meeting in the mountains.

The Soviet government usually allows one registered Protestant church per city to remain open, and many Russian Christians meet in these church buildings. However, thousands of Christians, like the believers in this story, gather in homes or in the forest to worship God. Sometimes they are forced to worship in homes or in the forest because there is no registered church in their city. In other instances, the one registered or open church in a city is not large enough to contain all the Christians who want to come.

For example, Moscow, a city of seven million, has one registered church. In Leningrad there is one Protestant church on the outskirts of the city to serve four million people.

Some Russian Christians choose to meet outside the registered church because they object to certain government restrictions on officially recognized churches. This government pressure against the church varies from year to year and also within different sections of the Soviet Union.

In some areas of Russia, Christians meet more freely. A Christian mother in the Ukraine told us, "Compared to the time of Stalin, we Christians in our city feel that now we have freedom."

But periodically in other parts of the U.S.S.R. the persecution of believers is severe. It is reliably estimated that there are still some 1,200 labor camps in the Soviet Union holding approximately one million people. Documents confirm that about 200 of these prisoners are Evangelical Christians.

The vast majority of Russia's estimated six million Protestant Christians are not in prison. But, like the Makarovitches, all Christian families in the Soviet Union face persecution in some measure simply because they are *verruyuschiye*—believers.

The Soviet government, for example, is adamantly opposed to Christian education of children. Although Article 124 of the Soviet constitution guarantees freedom of religion, other Soviet legislation makes it illegal for Christian young people under the age of 18 to gather officially for religious meetings.

In the story of Alexi's Secret Mission in Siberia, the children are censured as disloyal citizens by their teachers because they will not join the atheistic Young Pioneers communist youth club. When the policemen discover the youth meeting on Belovat Mountain, they are furious that young people should choose to be Christian "fanatics" like their parents.

In some instances, the pressure against Christian children in Soviet schools has become so intense that Russian parents have publicized their complaints in *samizdat* (self-published documents) that have been smuggled to the West.

In Barnaul, Siberia, for example, Christian children were persecuted so relentlessly that many of the Christian parents removed their children from school in 1971 and refused to send them back until the situation improved a year later.

In a document from Russia, the parents of Barnaul describe their predicament:

> It was especially difficult for our children in the schools where they read lectures on atheism. In these lectures the professors poured out their

wrath upon the Christian children who were present in the classroom. The lectures were intended to humiliate and hurt the students . . . .

Also, the Christian students were questioned separately and personally about the activities of their parents and other adult Christians. This was done forcibly against the will of the children and it is always done without the presence of the parents.

Here is one example: In one Soviet school where there are an exceptionally large number of Christian children studying, a Soviet government investigator by the name of Shtirov came. As Christians in Barnaul, we were acquainted with him from earlier encounters that we had had with him.

He held private investigations at the school in a separate room, calling in the Christian children one at a time. One Christian boy who didn't want to go to this investigation was dragged from the classroom by his legs down a staircase so that his head bounced down every stair as they dragged him to the investigating room. However, in the course of the questioning, the boy was able to run away and escape from Mr. Shtirov.

The second boy that was questioned was interrogated right in his classroom in front of the entire class and in the presence of his teacher. During the investigation, the attention of the investigator and teacher were distracted. When they turned their heads the Christian boy ran out of the classroom and hid in a room somewhere else in the building.

When we parents of these Christian children later learned of these incidents, we all came together as a group to the school to protest. We arrived at the school while the investigation was still taking place. However, when Mr. Shtirov saw us coming, he stopped the questioning and said it would continue another time in the future.

Because of this, as of March 16, 1972, we Christian parents decided to withdraw all of our children from school. From that time on, we did not allow them to return to the classrooms. We said to the teachers, "If this is the way our children are going to be treated, then we will not allow them to go to school any longer."

Of course, our children were extremely frightened and didn't say anything during the questioning . . . . They were asked such questions as: "Do you believe in God? Who taught you to believe? Do you pray? Where did you see God? Do you attend church? Who directs the church meetings? Who preaches at the church meetings? Do you have a Sunday school at church for children? Who among the adults conducts the Sunday school and youth meetings? How many children attend the church services? Whose children are they—what are their names? Who conducts the children's meetings?" and other similar questions.

If the investigators had been able to get the right answers to these questions, this information would have convicted our Christian adults and would have been used to sentence them for three to five years in prison.

During 1973, the situation apparently improved, and the Christian parents of Barnaul allowed their children to return to the local Soviet school.

But the struggle of Christians in the atheistic Soviet Union is not over. In July, 1973, Christians wrote the following from Barnaul, "The future griefs and persecutions awaiting Christians can be imagined by reading the new law on national education. This aims at completely excluding religious influence in the education of children."

In the battle to survive in an atheistic society, Russian Christians face overwhelming odds. But they are not defeated. Persistently and wisely they follow Christ and share their faith with others.

They often cite a favorite passage of Scripture which describes their situation: "For we preach not ourselves, but Christ Jesus the Lord; and ourselves your servants for Jesus' sake. We are troubled on every side, yet not distressed; we are perplexed, but not in despair; persecuted, but not forsaken; cast down, but not destroyed" (II Cor. 4:5, 8, 9).